The Artorian Chronicles

Nicholas Mrvos

A9 Publishing

ISBN: 979-8-234-01557-0
Printed in the United States of America

Cover design by [Alice Grace]

The Artorian Chronicles

TABLE OF Contents

Chapter 1

SHATTERED SIGNAL

Except for the movement of her fingers across the holographic console that hovered before her like a constellation of data points, Dr. Alyssa Artoria stood nearly still. Her eyes were locked on the stream of data from the deep-space telescopes, while the observation deck of Luna Station offered an unhindered view of the velvet expanse of space. The air smelled faintly of ozone and sterilized metal, the scent of machines that had long replaced flowers. The hum of the station vibrated through her boots, a steady heartbeat of human presence in the void.

She whispered, “Come on, show me you’re real,” her voice barely louder than the circuitry.

The signal was faint, barely distinguishable in the cosmic winds, but its rhythm and constancy stood out against the universe’s chaos. A possible lighthouse from a planet hidden in the habitable zone of a distant star. As she combed through the data, her focus remained unbroken.

One final tap locked the sequence in place. The numbers confirmed what her instincts already knew. It was time to center her work on this world.

The corner of her mouth lifted. "Let's not keep destiny waiting," she murmured.

Minutes later, Alyssa entered the main research lab in her clean blue uniform, the Luna Station insignia gleaming. A charged energy pulsed through the room.

"Team, gather," she called. Four heads turned, faces alert.

"Something significant has emerged from our deep-space sweep," she began, her tone touched with rare excitement.

She pointed to the hovering 3D projection.

"Here is a planet that could be humanity's next chapter."

The holographic globe shimmered to life above the table, swelling until it filled the room with soft light. Continents of deep emerald stretched across vast oceans, sapphire in color. Two pale moons orbited in tandem, casting ghostly reflections over cloud systems that coiled like living breath.

"Temperature?" asked Kellan, eyes wide.

"Seventeen degrees average," Alyssa replied, reading the data cascading down the side panel. "Oxygen near Earth-normal. Trace methane. Stable carbon cycle. Magnetosphere is strong."

Zara stepped closer, whispering, “That’s no dead rock. It’s alive.”

Alyssa nodded slowly. “Rotational tilt gives mild seasons, axial spin nearly perfect.”

She zoomed in, and the projection rotated, revealing glacial caps gleaming like crystalline mirrors at the poles. Equatorial regions glowed with hints of chlorophyll bands, plant-life analogs suggested by the spectral readings.

“Seismic data shows an active core,” Michael said, his breath catching. “That means plate movement. Weather patterns. A living cycle.”

“Stable magnetic readings,” Elena added quietly. “It can sustain an atmosphere long-term.”

Alyssa’s gaze softened as the world turned slowly before them, veined with light and shadow. “This isn’t just another planet. It’s a world that waited.”

For a long moment, no one spoke. The only sound was the soft thrum of the holoprojector.

Finally, Michael broke the silence. “What do we call it?”

Zara smiled faintly. “It deserves a name worthy of the find.”

Kellan turned to Alyssa. “You found it, Doctor. It should carry your name.”

Alyssa hesitated, eyes still on the globe. “It doesn’t belong to me,” she said softly. “It belongs to all of us.”

“Then it’s fitting,” Zara replied. “Artoria, a name for a world that belongs to everyone.”

The word hung in the air, both gentle and immense.

Alyssa exhaled, the glow of the planet reflected in her eyes. “Artoria,” she whispered, as if accepting a vow, not an honor.

Gasps rippled through the team. They all recognized the enormity. This was not just another celestial body, but a promise, a hope for a species that had searched the heavens for generations.

“We are on the cusp of discovery,” Alyssa said. “Generations will benefit from the work we begin here.”

The team exchanged excited glances. Urgency charged the room. They were pioneers, explorers, scientists, driven to unlock the stars.

A quiet pride warmed Alyssa’s chest. This was more than science. It was history unfolding, and they would be its architects.

She directed her team with precision, her gaze fixed on the sweeping holographic screens. Graphs and numbers flickered across the translucent displays.

"Dr. Ward, refine the atmospheric model. I need certainty on those oxygen levels."

Kellan's fingers, faintly stained with sensor dye, drummed once on the edge of his console before flying over the keys. "On it," he said, lines of focus deepening between his brows.

"Zara, run another simulation on the gravitational field," Alyssa continued.

Zara adjusted the projection overlay with a practiced flick. "Initiating," she said, her tone clipped but confident. A smirk tugged briefly at her lips. "Let's hope gravity likes us back."

"Michael, Elena, geothermal analysis."

Michael leaned closer to the hologram, his tone soft with awe. "Active plate tectonics," he murmured. "It's alive down there."

Elena's reply was steady, precise, as if each syllable were calibrated. "Consistent with a stable climate system."

Each discovery stacked toward a conclusion that swelled in the air, like pressure before a storm.

"Confirmed. Artoria is habitable."

The word lingered, vast and irreversible. This was more than science. It was survival, the opening of a future humanity had nearly lost.

Alyssa exhaled. “My friends, we have found the new home of humanity. This moment will shape history.”

The news raced across the scientific community at the speed of transmission. Within hours, institutes on Earth and across the colonies buzzed with the data. At the Martian Geosurvey Institute, scientists whispered in awe, “We’ve found a new home.”

The name Artoria spread, no longer just a designation but a symbol of hope. Prominent academics issued statements. The chair of the Planetary Society praised Alyssa’s findings as “a monumental leap for colonization.” Universities planned symposiums. The UN Space Coalition convened emergency meetings.

To honor Alyssa and her team, Luna Station prepared a ceremony. The observation deck, normally a quiet haven, transformed into a theater of light and glass. Luna’s surface stretched beyond the panoramic windows as a silent witness. Rows of delegates, engineers, and dignitaries filled the seats, their faces illuminated by banners projected above them:

THE HORIZON INITIATIVE — HUMANITY’S NEXT CHAPTER.

Alyssa stood at the podium, hands resting on its edge. The faint vibration of the station’s power core thrummed through the floor beneath her boots, a heartbeat she could not quite ignore. Beyond the glass, the ship gleamed in dry dock, its metallic skin catching the cold sunlight.

"My colleagues," she began, her voice steady though her throat was dry, "for generations humanity has looked upward, asking if the stars would ever answer. Today, we learn that the question was never theirs to answer. It was always ours."

A soft murmur rippled through the audience. She met their eyes. They saw resolve. Only she felt the weight pressing behind her ribs.

"We have found a new world, Artoria, a planet that waits not to be conquered but understood. What we build, we carry there as guests, not masters."

The words were polished, but beneath them lay something raw. She could still smell the ozone from propulsion tests. The hum might one day turn fatal if a stabilizer slipped. How many in this crowd knew that the drive they celebrated was still one errant calculation away from disaster?

"This mission belongs to no one person, no single nation," she continued. "It belongs to the species that dared to hope when hope itself seemed outdated."

Applause rose like a wave, measured and reverent. Alyssa nodded and stepped back. The sound filled the chamber but left her untouched, her pulse still beating to the rhythm of engines instead of clapping hands. Lights from the observation windows caught her reflection, not the face of a hero, but a woman already half turned toward the stars. In the distance, the Horizon waited, silver against the black, silent, immense, and almost alive.

The room fell silent. Alyssa pointed to the largest hologram, a detailed model of a spacecraft that seemed to pulse with potential.

Tracing the outline of its engines, she said, "Propulsion is our first hurdle. Crossing interstellar distances in a timeframe that makes colonization viable requires something beyond fusion or ion drives."

The air vibrated faintly as containment rings hummed in standby. A tang of coolant mixed with the sterilized bite of recycled oxygen.

Dr. Zara Malik stepped forward, datapad under her arm, eyes catching the blue glow of the projection. "I've been modeling a hybrid system, the Alcubierre field engine stabilized by a quantum impulse array. The field bends spacetime itself. The array emits synchronized quantum bursts to keep the warp bubble intact."

Alyssa leaned closer, studying the simulation as light rippled across her face. The hologram shimmered, space folding like silk around a single glowing point. "And if the impulses fall out of sync?"

"Then the bubble collapses." Zara's tone stayed even, but her eyes betrayed a thrill. "One misfire, and the Horizon gets smeared across a light year."

A low hum rolled through the deck plating, deep and steady, as if the ship's unfinished heart had answered. The smell of ozone cut the air, static crawling along the displays.

"So," Kellan said, rubbing the bridge of his nose, "we're traveling inside a weaponized physics experiment."

Zara's mouth twitched. "Essentially. The Alcubierre field handles the heavy lifting. The quantum impulse array keeps spacetime from eating us."

Alyssa folded her arms. "Stabilization redundancy?"

"Three backup emitters," Zara replied. "But if the exotic matter field fluctuates, even backups won't hold. We'd have milliseconds before implosion."

Kellan frowned, his voice low. "We'd vanish between stars. No debris. No trace."

Alyssa studied the swirling model, the pulse of the warp bubble reflected in her eyes like a second heartbeat. "We'll reinforce the impulse control grid. Layer the failsafes. If this works, we won't just reach Artoria. We will change the boundaries of human reach."

Zara nodded, making quick annotations on her tablet. “I’ll adjust the emitter timing. It’s like threading quantum needles while the universe moves.”

“Do it,” Alyssa said. “And log everything. The Alcubierre field will carry us. The impulse array will keep us alive.”

Static crackled overhead. The hum faded to a deep bass vibration, then steadied. A momentary silence filled the chamber, charged and fragile.

“Beautiful,” Alyssa whispered. “And utterly terrifying.”

“Welcome to deep-space engineering,” Zara replied, a faint smile breaking through her composure.

Across the chamber, Dr. Kellan Ward studied the star-system projection, one hand absently running along his jawline as he calculated. “We’ll need to account for gravitational nuances in the Colonial 9 System,” he said. “Timing the insertion burn will be like threading a needle.”

Alyssa nodded, well aware that even slight miscalculations could be fatal. Her focus shifted to Dr. Elena Rivera, bent over life-support schematics.

“Oxygen generation looks strong,” Elena reported. She brushed a speck of lunar dust from her sleeve, a small gesture of control. “But I need algae bioreactors more resilient to temperature and light shifts.”

“Life is resilient,” Alyssa said gently. “Design your system to reflect that perseverance.”

Elena straightened, resolve renewed. “Exactly.”

Pride swelled in Alyssa as she surveyed her team. Here, in Luna Station’s steel-and-glass core, they were shaping humanity’s future.

“All right, everyone,” she called, drawing their focus. “Let’s make this ship worthy of the journey. We have a planet to reach and a legacy to build.”

Resolve deepened across the room. They were no longer just scientists. They were trailblazers.

With her palms pressed to the table, Alyssa leaned forward. The faces around her glowed in the holographic light.

Dr. Ward broke the silence. He rubbed at his temple, eyes scanning the propulsion readouts. “The propulsion system is revolutionary, but unproven on this scale. A journey across light-years with lives at stake is no small gamble.”

Dr. Michael Hale lifted his gaze from the cryostasis data. “Every risk reminds us why this matters,” he said quietly, his conviction soft but unshakable.

Alyssa raised a hand. Silence fell. “We knew this path would be risky. But we are not only scientists. We are stewards of humanity’s future. Every obstacle we overcome secures survival.”

Zara leaned in, her grin quick and fierce. “Then let’s make it the safest gamble in history.”

Elena’s reply followed with steady assurance. “Environmental controls are nearly ready,” she said. “The colonists will wake to sunrises like Earth’s.”

Alyssa rose, her tone lifting the room. “Together, we carry the torch to a new dawn. Preparation will meet every risk.”

Assent murmured around the chamber, binding them to a single purpose.

Weeks later, the first colonization ship prototype towered in Luna Station’s hangar, its hull gleaming under floodlights. Crowds gathered, eyes reflecting the promise etched into steel.

Alyssa, in her blue uniform, strode to the podium. “This is a pivotal day.”

Inside the planning room, she faced her team once more as risk assessments and trajectories hovered above them. “The trip to Artoria is full of unknowns. There are great risks, but also the chance our species may find a new cradle."

Kellan frowned. "Cryosleep is untested across such distances. We cannot predict the psychological toll."

Alyssa gestured toward Elena. "That's why we're doubling neural health simulations."

Zara tapped the propulsion schematics. "The engineering margins are thin. One mistake could strand us between stars."

"Our calculations won't be off," Alyssa answered, her eyes steady. "Every variable has been tested. We are ready for this leap. This will define our legacy."

A hush followed. Then nods spread like a tide.

Later, in the observation bay, Alyssa stood before dignitaries and station staff. Below them, the ship gleamed, unveiled at last.

"Behold, the S.S. Horizon," Alyssa said. Gasps rippled through the crowd.

She stepped closer to the glass, her reflection merging with the vessel. "This ship carries not just our hopes, but proof of human determination. Today we etch our names into history, not as those who shrink from the dark, but as torchbearers lighting the path to humanity's new home."

Applause thundered through the bay. Alyssa lifted her eyes to the stars, a silent promise burning in her gaze.

Back in the main lab, the hum of activity resumed.

Elena called out, “Oxygen scrubber efficiency is at ninety-eight point seven percent.”

“Push it to ninety-nine,” Alyssa replied. “We can’t gamble with air.”

Zara added, her eyes locked on equations that bent space. “I’m running another simulation on the Alcubierre drive.”

The containment coils pulsed faintly through the deck, a deep rhythmic thrum like the slow heartbeat of a restrained beast. Pale light flickered across Zara’s face as the holographic readouts shimmered, showing the faint distortion of folded space.

Without raising his gaze, Kellan advised, “Watch the distribution of exotic matter. The quantum impulse timing has to stay perfect.”

“Understood,” Zara said, adjusting the stabilizer frequencies. “If the impulses slip even by a breath, the field tears itself apart. But not this time.”

Static whispered across the consoles, the faint scent of ozone curling through the recycled air. Alyssa watched in silence as the simulation steadied, the shimmering bubble holding form for several seconds longer than before.

"Field stability at ninety-four percent," Zara reported, her voice calm but clipped. "The array's syncing cleaner with each pass."

"Good," Alyssa said. "Let's keep the Horizon intact at least until lunch."

A ripple of quiet laughter passed through the lab, cutting the tension. For a heartbeat, the hum of the drive sounded less like a threat and more like a promise.

They were a team, bound by the gravity of their mission, their focus orbiting Alyssa's leadership. Camaraderie moved through the room like a steady current.

"Final launch sequence is locked," Michael called, the words heavy with meaning.

Alyssa turned to her team. "Then it's time. Gather the colonists."

She stood before them in the assembly hall, her blue uniform immaculate, her silver-streaked hair a testament to decades of service. Clearing her throat, she commanded silence. Scientists, engineers, and future residents of Artoria filled the chamber, united by the dream of a new beginning.

"Today is not an end, but a beginning," she said, her voice carrying both gravity and hope. "The trip to Artoria will be difficult. Beyond the obstacles lies a living world that can host humanity's renewal."

Her words settled over the room, her perceptive gaze noting the mix of fear and anticipation etched on every face.

"Artoria offers more than a home. It gives us the chance to learn from Earth's past, to grow, adapt, and live in harmony with a new world." Her voice rose. "Our mission is born from generations who looked to the stars and dreamed. It is our honor to carry their journey forward."

Applause erupted, echoing like the roar of engines soon to launch them into the void.

With her voice as steady as a compass, Alyssa concluded, "Let us begin this odyssey with clear minds and full hearts. Artoria awaits the dawn of our future."

Her words drew a standing ovation, a thunderous confirmation of their trust in her, a promise she intended to honor at any cost.

From a walkway above the concourse, Alyssa watched as personnel and colonists bustled below with purposeful urgency. Luna Station vibrated with activity. Cargo drones hummed along fixed paths, ferrying supplies to ships, their sleek frames the result of countless hours of labor.

Everywhere she looked, people moved with intent. Scientists calibrated instruments. Engineers ran system checks. Families embraced, tears mixing with the spark of new beginnings. Children clutched hand-drawn pictures of Artoria, their imaginations already painting the green world they would soon call home.

"Look, Mom," a boy cried, tugging at his mother's sleeve. "That's where we're going, right. The new world?"

"Yes, sweetheart," she answered, smiling bravely despite the tremor in her voice. "Our future lies there."

The weight of legacy pressed on Alyssa as her gaze lingered on the family.

She turned and walked to the observation deck, where Luna's gray regolith fell away to the velvet dark of space. The faint glimmer of the Colonial 9 System, visible only through the station's telescopes yet fixed in her mind, called to her.

The deck was nearly dark, lit only by the soft shimmer of control panels and the distant curve of Luna beneath her feet. The air carried a trace of coolant and cold glass. She pressed her hands to the railing, feeling its chill seep through her gloves. The distant thrum of engines preparing for another test resonated through the deck, a promise of motion beneath the silence.

Somewhere out there, barely visible, waited the world that now bore her name. Artoria.

She imagined its twin moons rising over forests untouched by industry, rivers threading through valleys where no human sound had ever traveled. The thought should have calmed her. Instead, it set her pulse racing.

In her mind's eye, the holographic globe still turned. Emerald continents. Sapphire seas. Swirling clouds like slow breaths. It was beautiful, yes, but the beauty carried weight. For all their simulations and stabilizers, they still did not know what waited below those clouds.

A tremor from the engines thrummed through the hull. The Alcubierre containment coils were warming for another test, or perhaps the ship was simply responding to the distance ahead.

Alyssa drew in a slow breath, the recycled air tasting faintly of metal and ozone. "Soon," she whispered, not to herself, but to the dark beyond the glass.

The stars did not answer. They only burned, patient and indifferent, as if daring her to reach them.

Behind her, the faint vibration deepened, the sound of power waiting to be unleashed.

And in that moment, standing between Earth's moon and the promise of another world, Dr. Alyssa Artoria felt the future tilt forward, ready to begin.

Chapter 2

ECHOES OF COMMAND

There was a tangible tension in the spacecraft, an electric charge of anticipation that made the colonists' spines tingle. Amid the anxious energy, Dr. Alyssa Artoria stood as a steady anchor. She reassured each pair of eyes with her steady gaze. Liora, calm but wide-eyed, sought the reassurance of her mother's presence.

With the precision of her scientific mind and the warmth of a leader who had guided them through fire and stardust alike, Alyssa's voice cut through the whispers. "This is not an end but a beginning. We are the architects of our future on Artoria." Her words settled over the cabin with the weight of a promise.

Liora nodded, drawing strength from her mother's poise. Alyssa squeezed her daughter's hand, a silent vow to face the future together.

The countdown echoed like a heartbeat. When the call came, "Ignition," the outside world blurred into sound and motion.

With a thunderous roar, the engines came alive, shaking the ship's frame. As human ingenuity lifted them from Earth's cradle, vibrations swept through the floor, climbed their legs, and pressed against their chests.

Pinned to her acceleration couch, Alyssa felt the weight settle like an unseen force on her chest. Colonists clung to armrests, faces caught between fear and excitement. As they surrendered to the journey beyond the only home they had known, mouths opened in gasps and eyes squeezed shut.

The spacecraft rose, an arrow piercing the atmosphere and breaking free into the vast emptiness of space. Earth shrank beneath them, a swirling marble of green and blue veiled in white.

Alyssa smiled, her expression shaped by years of stargazing, as Liora's grip tightened. She whispered, "Look ahead, my star. We're traveling straight into history."

Silence followed, deep and total, as the last traces of Earth vanished. A collective exhale carried awe at the enormity of their leap. The thought of what lay ahead, a world that would test their resolve, set Alyssa's heart racing.

She looked at her daughter, at the crew, and at the people who had left everything behind, making a quiet promise to lead them to a dawn unseen, on the shores of an emerald world.

In contrast to their roaring ascent, the ship now drifted in the quiet of space. The colonists adapted to cramped quarters, recycled air, and the constant vibration that reminded them of their relentless velocity through the void.

With practiced ease, Dr. Alyssa Artoria moved through the narrow corridors, her body tuned to microgravity. She paused at a viewport, where distant stars shone indifferently. She shifted her focus from the infinite outside to the men and women who depended on her leadership.

"Conserve movement. Every gesture must be purposeful," she told a group of engineers studying a schematic. They nodded, absorbing her guidance without question.

One engineer reported, "Dr. Artoria" oxygen scrubbers are optimal, but once we land, the dust could create problems we can't predict."

"Good point, Carter," Alyssa replied, already assembling solutions in her mind. "Redundancy is our ally. Draft a schedule with extra cleanings."

At the next console, Dr. Kellan Ward adjusted a simulation readout, his brow furrowed. "Pressure curves are steady, but if Mars throws another dust front as the last report predicted, we'll need to modify descent models."

Alyssa nodded approvingly. "Flag it for the atmospheric systems log. I want redundancy layered on redundancy."

Liora quietly admired her mother. The silver in Alyssa's hair seemed less a mark of age than a symbol of earned authority, almost otherworldly in the context of their voyage.

Time in space flowed strangely until at last descent approached. Screens glowed with diagnostics and trajectories, the control room alive with tension. Alyssa stood beside the pilots, eyes fixed on the flashing data.

"Initiate deceleration sequence," she ordered. The pilots' hands moved with practiced precision across the controls.

"Approaching atmospheric entry," one pilot announced, breaking the silence. Metal groaned as the ship fought against Mars' thin atmosphere.

"Keep her steady," Alyssa commanded, masking the unease twisting in her stomach. "We can't risk a bounce-back trajectory. Adjust angle of descent to zero point three degrees."

The pilots' focus never wavered as sweat beaded on their foreheads. Outside, flames streamed along the hull like those of a phoenix, cutting through the sky.

The callouts came fast, the surface racing to meet them. "Altitude forty thousand, thirty, twenty."

With her eyes on the altimeter, Alyssa ordered, "Deploy landing gear." The legs extended, confirmed by the heavy clunk of machinery.

Just before impact, she added, "Thrusters to stabilize." The craft trembled violently as it landed, drawing gasps from the cabin.

Alyssa let the ghost of a smile pass her lips. "Touchdown confirmed. Welcome to Mars." Relief and awe rippled through the crew.

Liora touched her mother's shoulder. "You did it, Mom. We made it."

Alyssa corrected gently, "We did it." Pride swelled in her chest for herself, her daughter, and everyone who had dared to hope for this start. Together, they had written a new chapter in human exploration.

A soft chime pulsed on Alyssa's wrist screen, a mission log update. "Mars Base Alpha, operational confirmation received," it read. Her eyes lingered on the next line. "This site remains the proving ground before Artoria.

The S.S. Horizon awaits completion of Alcubierre alignment at Luna Station." It steadied her heart to see it in text, a reminder that this was not the destination, but the test.

A hiss of air mingled with the thin atmosphere as the hatch opened. For a moment, Dr. Alyssa Artoria stood at the threshold, gazing at crimson earth and ochre dunes. No solace of blue sky, only a pale, butterscotch horizon. This was Mars, stark, unforgiving, yet waiting.

"Remember," she whispered, more to herself than the others, "every step is a victory."

She descended the ramp, boots crunching on gravelly regolith. Liora followed close behind, suits shielding them from the cold, their breaths loud in their helmets, a reminder of the life they carried into this emptiness.

One by one, colonists emerged, eyes wide with awe and edged with fear. No simulation had prepared them for the reality of standing on another world.

Liora's voice cut through the comms. "Don't get lost in the view. We have work to do."

A flicker of pride crossed Alyssa's expression. Her daughter's tone already carried command, measured, firm, unshaken. She remembered Craig Hefner's training words from Luna Station, that leadership was contagious when modeled, not declared.

Alyssa watched her daughter step into leadership with poise beyond her years. The group worked quickly to unload prefabricated panels and supports. Designed for fast assembly, the shelters strained against the plains' rough winds.

Alyssa rushed to aid an engineer whose module caught the wind like a sail. "Secure that panel," she shouted, her gloved hands moving with practiced ease.

Zara Malik appeared beside her, wind roaring through the comms. "Got it, locking clamp," she shouted. Sparks flickered as the fastener sealed. "If this wind keeps up, I'm naming this storm after you, "Dr. Artoria." She laughed, then added, more quietly, "At least it's not water. I always hated the ocean."

Alyssa huffed a laugh. "Then make sure I outlast it."

Even behind his mask, the engineer's gratitude was clear. "Good catch, "Dr. Artoria."

She gave a quick nod and moved on.

"Mom, tethering duty," Liora called, pointing to supply crates at risk of scattering. "Our rations can't travel the planet without us."

Alyssa clipped tethers from her belt. "Copy that." The work was tedious, far from research papers and equations, but every action mattered. Survival depended on it.

By nightfall, shelters held firm against the cold. Long shadows stretched across their fragile colony. Alyssa paused as the last light touched the domes, taking in what they had built.

Liora joined her. "First night on Mars," she said, grinning. "Camping back home isn't the same."

Alyssa put an arm around her shoulders. "Home is where we make it. And this is home, for now."

She didn't mention that the base had existed for years, barely habitable, an outpost of failures and near abandonment. Mars had broken many crews before this one. But now the planet would serve its purpose, humanity's test field before Artoria.

Liora joked, "Then let's hope it's a welcoming one," but her eyes lingered on the fading skyline, as though seeking a star to wish upon, a fragile hope in an unknowable universe.

The storm came without mercy. Dust raged against the temporary command center, clawing at the colony's walls. Alyssa's visor blurred with red grit. They had not prepared for such intensity, and the gale threatened to undo their work.

A panel began to give way. “Seal that breach,” Alyssa’s voice cut through the chaos. Engineers rushed forward, huddled against the wind, their hands moving over Earth-forged tools now baptized in Martian dust.

Static crackled in her ear, the taste of iron flooding her mouth through the recycled air. Kellan’s voice broke through the interference. “Pressure’s dropping fast, gusts at one hundred forty meters per second.”

“Zara, lock down the greenhouse conduits,” Alyssa ordered. “Elena, reroute heat flow to the shelters. Prioritize life support.”

Through the storm, Liora’s voice cried, “Mother. There’s a jam in Shelter C’s airlock.”

“Divert power from non-essential systems,” Alyssa ordered. Her mind worked like a conductor guiding survival. “I’ll handle it.”

She forced her way through the storm, servos whining under pressure. Grit pounded her suit, each grain carving against their new home.

At last, the airlock yielded, revealing colonists trapped inside. One engineer shouted, “Got it.” Alyssa caught their relieved nods, though the storm’s roar swallowed their sighs.

Michael Hale stumbled out beside them, coughing through static. “First time I’ve seen a planet try to kill me before breakfast.”

Alyssa clapped his shoulder. “Welcome to Mars.”

When the storm passed, silence revealed the damage, cut comm lines, scarred solar panels, and equipment buried in sand. They had endured their first true test at a cost.

“Let’s get to it,” Alyssa said firmly. “We survive. We reinforce. We repair.”

“And next time,” Zara muttered, brushing sand from her helmet, “we design storm shutters that don’t flirt with disaster.”

Alyssa allowed herself a small smile. “Add it to the list.”

But water soon became their greatest trial. The drilling rigs, meant to pierce ice and rock, stalled repeatedly in thick regolith.

“Adjust thermal exchange ratio,” Alyssa said, crouched over pipes and sensors. “Recalibrate for these conditions.”

“Dr. Artoria”, we’ve tried everything in the manual,” an engineer sighed.

“That’s because Mars didn’t read the manual,” Zara quipped, tapping her wristpad. “Try lowering the pulse frequency to two point two hertz. Kellan, can you model the pressure feedback loop in real time?"

Kellan frowned, his brow slick with sweat beneath his helmet. "Already on it. But if this drill overheats, we'll vaporize the water table before we ever touch it."

"Then cool the system with external venting," Michael Hale countered, his voice steady but tired. "It'll slow our progress, but we'll preserve structural integrity."

Elena's calm voice broke through the comms from inside the habitat. "Environmental sensors show a chemical imbalance. Trace methane is spiking around the drill site. Be careful. One spark, and we'll ignite the soil."

Alyssa took it all in, directing the moment like a conductor guiding survival. "Then we stabilize. No sparks. No shortcuts. Zara, your venting plan stands. Michael, recalibrate the heating curve by zero point zero three."

Her fingers flew across the console, eyes narrowing as readings danced before her.

"Then we rewrite the manual," she said, her tone firm. Her fingers continued across the screen, eyes searching for variables in the maze of data. "Mars won't give up its secrets easily. We adapt, or we fail."

Days passed in trial and error. At last, the drill sputtered to life, and a stream of salty water spurted from the ground. The exhausted crew erupted in cheers.

Alyssa allowed a fleeting smile. “Sample it. Filter it. Make sure it’s fit.” This was only the first of many victories, but perseverance had won them water.

Zara’s laughter crackled over the comms. “It’s ugly, and it smells like rust, but it’s ours.”

Colonists gathered, hope bright in their eyes. “Brilliant, Mom,” Liora said.

“Science, Liora,” Alyssa corrected gently, her gaze drifting toward the Horizon. “And Martian perseverance.”

Still, loneliness weighed heavily. Alyssa watched colonists drift through makeshift passageways, dust clinging to their suits as a constant reminder. She overheard fragments of homesick whispers.

A young botanist muttered, “Sometimes I can’t believe we’re millions of miles from everything we knew.”

“Stay focused on why we’re here. We are the vanguard of humanity,” Alyssa said, calm but sympathetic.

The botanist tried to smile. “Easy for you to say, “Dr. Artoria”.You have Liora.”

Nearby, Liora looked up from her maintenance schedule, exchanging a quiet nod with her mother. Both understood their duty, not only to lead, but to steady morale.

Alyssa guided the botanist toward the greenhouse domes gleaming in weak light. “Let’s check the plants.”

Inside, the atmosphere changed. Green leaves stirred in the artificial breeze, oxygen-rich air washing over them. Rows of seedlings promised self-sufficiency.

Alyssa brushed a tomato sprout. “Life support is more than machines. Every seedling brings us closer to independence. They are our bridge to sustainability.”

“She’s right,” Liora added. “Every harvest proves we can thrive, not just survive. It boosts morale more than any pep talk.”

Alyssa watched her daughter adjust a nutrient feed, impressed by her ability to shift from strategy to hands-on work. Adaptability was what kept them alive.

Liora pointed at spinach-like leaves. “Look, Mom. They’re thriving, even with less light. Our genetic work is paying off.”

“Brilliant,” Alyssa whispered, pride swelling not only for the science but also for Liora’s perseverance and the team’s shared resolve. One breath, one meal at a time, they were building a home.

"Dr. Rivera," Alyssa called across the greenhouse, "check the oxygen curve again."

Elena's voice came back through the static. "Slight dip in CO_2 conversion. Filters might need backflushing. I'll handle it."

Alyssa nodded, though the tightness in her chest remained. Every breath here depended on machinery and fragile balance. One miscalibration, and life would vanish as quickly as breath on glass.

"Come on," Liora urged. "They need good news. Let's share it."

The green oasis gave way to plastic and steel corridors as they walked back to the colony's center. Their unspoken vow to persevere, to build, to endure, showed in every step.

At the forefront of the gathered crowd, Alyssa faced the weary colonists. Supplies were running low, and she saw it in their drawn faces, sleepless eyes, and worry-creased brows.

"We stand on the brink of a new era," she declared, her voice steady. "Every day we take strides. Every challenge proves our resilience."

Hope flickered across the crowd. Murmurs spread, heads nodding slowly. Alyssa's calm conviction lifted them.

"Everyone of you has a role," she continued. "Now more than ever, unity matters. Share your ideas, no matter how small. Together, we will find our strength."

Her gaze shifted toward the medical wing, where Dr. Singh, the lead physician, waited. The news was grim. A virus, harmless on Earth, had breached the colony's defenses.

Singh's voice was low, roughened by exhaustion. "It's spreading fast. What's harmless at one gravity seems to be mutating under partial gravity." He glanced at his tablet. "Low fevers, respiratory distress, early dehydration. I've isolated ten so far."

"Start full containment protocols," Alyssa ordered. "No one moves between sectors without sterilization."

Despite her worry, Alyssa entered with clinical focus. The antiseptic hum of machines was broken by coughing patients crowding the cots. Shadows from monitors flickered across her face as she moved among the sick.

"Double-check filtration," she told a technician, her calm voice edged with command. "No cross-contamination. Sanitize every surface again."

"Dr. Artoria" a nurse said, her face tense with anxiety. "If more people get sick, our antiviral supplies will run low."

Alyssa nodded, firm. "Then we'll prioritize treatment by severity. Get creative. Start synthesizing more from the raw materials we have left."

Dr. Singh met her gaze. "I'll work with Zara. She's already got the power grid stabilized for the med lab. Maybe we can repurpose some nano filters from the water rigs to catch viral particulates."

"Do it," Alyssa said.

"Mom?" Liora's voice cut through the tension. Alyssa turned to face her daughter, the weight of responsibility etched on both their faces.

"Let's go outside," Alyssa said, guiding her daughter into the bleak Martian night. Side by side, they looked at the colony buildings standing like silent sentinels.

"Leadership is hardest when the air's thin," Alyssa said softly. "When you feel like there's not enough to breathe, you have to give what you have left."

"Mom, I've never seen an outbreak spread so quickly," Liora admitted, her voice trembling.

"Nor have I," Alyssa said, eyes fixed on the Horizon where the dim blue glow of Earth was visible. "But we've faced unknowns before. We adjust and overcome."

Liora's voice trailed. "Even if it means…" She couldn't finish.

"Even if," Alyssa confirmed, placing a hand on her daughter's shoulder. "But this mission is about more than survival. It's about giving humanity a future. And we'll do everything in our power to make sure that happens."

When Liora looked into her mother's eyes, she saw the same determination that had inspired so many others. "Then we continue. For everyone at home, for those who gaze at the stars and dream."

The connection between them was as real as the cold Martian air. They carried not only the burden of leadership but also the spirit that had held humanity this far. Together, they returned to the colony, where so many depended on them.

Inside, Alyssa put her arm around Liora and said, "Come on. Let's work together to find a solution."

In the communal dining area, Alyssa moved with ease through the crowd, her presence a quiet beacon of solidarity. The feast was inadequate by Earth standards, but a celebration of survival here. The makeshift tables held what rations could be spared. As stories filled the air and mingled with the aroma of rehydrated meals, faces weary from work and anxious about the outbreak softened into tentative smiles.

The low hum of the hydroponic fans mixed with laughter, a fragile symphony that made the habitat feel alive again. Somewhere in the background, Zara cursed softly at a flickering power conduit before earning applause when the lights steadied. "You're welcome," she muttered, pretending to bow. Even small victories mattered here.

Laughter burst out when an engineer joked, "Remember when we thought gravity boots would be the hardest adjustment?"

Another added with wonder, "Or the first time we saw a Martian sunset and thought it was an optical illusion?"

Dr. Michael Hale raised his cup of recycled water. "To impossible sunsets and drills that only break twice a day." The toast earned groans and cheers alike.

Alyssa sat next to Liora, picking at her food while listening more than eating. This was their family now, a community bound by shared risk and fragile hope. Sickness and fear could not erase the resolve shining in their eyes.

"Mom," Liora said, nudging her, "share your theory, the one about Earth seeds and Martian dust."

Alyssa stood with a knowing smile, capturing the room's attention. "It's more than a theory now," she said, describing a future where plants from Earth grew in Martian soil. "It's the beginning of transformation. Two worlds learning from each other, growing together."

Elena Rivera listened from the far end of the table, nodding thoughtfully. "If we can maintain stable oxygen from those hybrid crops, we might double our atmospheric output before the next supply run."

Kellan scribbled figures onto a tablet beside her, half amused, half inspired. "Assuming Zara doesn't short out the irrigation circuits again."

"One time," Zara said, mock glare cutting through laughter. "One damn time."

The colonists listened in awe as Alyssa's vision for humanity's future unfolded. For those who had left everything to begin anew, it was a story of perseverance and belonging in the vastness of space.

Even Dr. Singh, pale from exhaustion, stood near the back, his arms folded. "If we survive the week," he murmured, "I'll believe anything."

Alyssa caught his eye and nodded, a silent promise that belief was not optional here; it was survival.

Later, Alyssa left the habitat as the meal wound down, the Martian terrain stretching before her like an empty canvas. She looked up at the dark sky, where stars glowed. There was no Earthly horizon, only the infinity of space and the quiet ambition of those who dared explore it. For a fleeting moment, she longed for the gentle patter of Earth's rain on her skin, something Mars could never offer.

The cold air rasped against her helmet filter. Each inhale tasted faintly metallic. She glanced back at the domes glowing amber against the red plain, tiny islands of light in an ocean of dust.

Alone, Alyssa felt the enormity of their journey and the weight of responsibility. Yet opportunity pressed at her heart. They braved the unknown not just for themselves, but for all humanity. They were pioneers.

"Here we are at the edge of possibility," she whispered, a prayer to the sky.

A faint comm signal cracked in her ear, Liora checking in. "All quiet inside, Mom. Singh says symptoms are stabilizing. Looks like containment's working."

Alyssa exhaled, letting the tension leak from her chest. "Good," she whispered. "Tell him to rest. He's earned it."

A gentle wind stirred the dust at her boots, and Alyssa took it as confirmation that they belonged here. She drew a deep breath of thin air and turned back toward the colony, her silhouette stark against the reddening sky.

"Tomorrow," she said quietly, "we start again."

As Dr. Alyssa Artoria took the stage, the sound of hydroponic fans mingled with nervous voices. She looked out at the faces before her, all marked with the same somber understanding. The storage units, normally glowing blue, flickered erratically, raising doubts about their food supply's future.

"Everyone, please," she said, breaking through the clamor of concern. "I know you're worried about our provisions. The recent crop failure has put us in a precarious position, and our reserves are running out faster than we expected."

The colonists seemed to hold their breath, waiting for the assurance they had come to expect from their astrophysicist leader. In the face of hardship, Alyssa's composed manner remained a steady point of calm.

"But remember," she added, "we are pioneers on the frontier of human endurance. Together, we have transformed barren rock into a testament to our resolve."

She pointed to the window, where the red dust of Mars clung to the glass. With her eyes searching the room, she said, “We may need to ration more strictly and find new ways to maximize greenhouse outputs, but we will persevere.”

“Dr. Rivera and I are revising nutrient cycles,” she continued, her voice strong. “Kellan’s modeling the next storm season so we can protect our crops better this time. Every mind here counts.”

As the crowd began to nod, a cough, then another, and finally a moan came from the rear. For days, the symptoms had been growing more noticeable, and rumors of fever and exhaustion were spreading.

“Dr. Artoria” turned her focus to the community’s health concerns. “We are keeping a careful eye on the situation, and our medical team is working tirelessly to provide care and contain the illness.”

Dr. Singh rose weakly, mask dangling at his throat. “We’ve made progress synthesizing antivirals,” he said hoarsely. “Using compounds from the greenhouse roots. Crude, but promising.”

Applause rippled through the room, small but sincere.

She left the stage and went to the infirmary, where the antiseptic smell could not mask the underlying fear. With steely resolve and hidden dread, Liora stood beside a small child's cot. The two locked eyes and silently offered each other support.

Despite the gravity of her words, Liora's voice was steady as she reported, "Mother, we've isolated those showing symptoms, but our antiviral supplies are running low."

Alyssa's mind spun with possible answers. "Then we must do more with less," she said. "I'll work on the molecular breakdown and recombination. Start synthesizing what we can from local materials."

"Understood," Liora replied, admiring her mother's unblinking focus.

Dr. Singh approached, exhaustion etched deep. "It's working, Alyssa," he murmured, showing her the data. "Fever durations are shorter. We might have stopped it from mutating again." Alyssa allowed herself one measured breath of relief before returning to work.

They moved among the beds together, offering comfort to the sick and guidance to the healthy. "Dr. Artoria's "presence soothed the room, her steady steps and quiet touches easing anxious hearts.

With a voice both firm and compassionate, Alyssa advised a colonist, "Stay within the habitation zones and stay hydrated. Above all, keep hope alive. We are strong, and this is just another challenge on our path to a sustainable future here on Mars."

Her words lifted the community, and their leader's strength steadied them. Despite the threat of an outbreak, the colonists' resolve held firm, bolstered by Dr. Alyssa Artoria's commitment to finding answers.

Her eyes lingered on the diminishing readouts of the life-support reserves. The hum of machinery in her temporary office was a constant reminder of how fragile their balance remained.

"Mother," Liora whispered from the doorway.

The worried lines on Alyssa's face softened as she looked at her daughter. "Yes, darling?"

Liora stepped forward, weariness plain in her movements. "The new filtration units in the greenhouses aren't producing the desired results."

"Another setback," Alyssa muttered. She crossed the room to stand with her daughter. They exchanged a long glance, a language of fortitude shaped by years of shared impossibility.

Alyssa squeezed Liora's hand. "We've come this far, and I refuse to let our dream fade like dust in the Martian winds. We knew a foothold here would test every part of us."

Liora's voice faltered. "Challenges we anticipated, but this, Mother, it's unrelenting. The crew is afraid. If we don't change…"

"We will," Alyssa said firmly, tightening her grip. "The best thing humanity can do, the thing that carries us forward, is to innovate and adapt."

Her tone softened. "And the best leaders know when to listen. Take Zara tomorrow. She's been pushing for a power reroute to heat the soil faster. Meet with her, weigh it, then decide. Leadership isn't command. It's calibration."

Strengthened by her mother's belief, Liora nodded. Together, they walked out into the common space where colonists had gathered.

Before them was an improvised meal, hydroponically grown vegetables, and rationed supplies. The laughter and conversation that rose despite the hardships revealed the group's enduring spirit.

As he broke a piece of flatbread, one colonist asked, "Remember when we first landed? I assumed by now we'd be eating Martian potatoes, not algae supplements."

Another added, “Yet here we are, making do. Mars hasn’t defeated us yet if we can laugh about it.”

“Not yet,” Zara replied from across the table, smirking. “But it keeps trying.” Her comment earned a round of chuckles that warmed the cold metal walls.

As Liora joined the group, Alyssa saw how naturally her daughter’s leadership drew people in. They shared tales of Earth and their journey, each story tightening the bonds of the community.

A voice shouted, “Here’s to “Dr. Artoria,” raising a repurposed cup. “To Liora. To all of us. We’re trailblazers, creators of a new world.”

The chorus responded, “Hear, hear.” Their voices rose together, echoing against the bleak surroundings.

Alyssa allowed herself a small smile, finding solace in her people’s unity. She heard the resilience of humanity in their laughter and voices. It spread warmth through the room, pushing back the shadow of hopelessness that threatened their sanctuary on Mars.

They were more than survivors tonight. Against the odds, they remained a family, united by a shared goal, clinging to one another and to hope.

Dr. Alyssa Artoria sat alone in the dining room after the colonists had left, bringing the communal meal to an end.

With deliberate movements, she gathered the remaining utensils, each clink of metal against the tray sharp in the hollow space. A ritual of normalcy amid uncertainty.

As Alyssa stepped outside, the warm artificial light gave way to the faint glow of Mars' twin moons. Above her, the sky stretched black and endless, pierced by bursts of starlight. Fine dust drifted in the thin air and whispered against her suit.

She paused, hearing the faint pulse of life-support pumps through the ground, a heartbeat beneath her boots. The colony lived, however fragile, because they refused to stop.

She looked up, following the smaller moon's arc as it trailed its larger sibling. She felt the weight of far-off Earth, Luna Station, all they had left behind, and all that was yet to come. Here, beneath the Martian sky, she permitted herself to reflect.

Alyssa's breath fogged her visor, briefly veiling her view. When it cleared, her resolve held firm. What had once felt like a void of unknowns now hinted at possibility, a future beyond their birth world.

"New beginnings," she whispered, barely audible above the hum in her helmet. It was her mantra, born of decades of study, failures, and victories. Now it fueled her and her people as they carried humanity toward Artoria.

Liora's earlier words returned. "We chart the course not by stars already known, but by those yet to be discovered." Alyssa knew their mission was not just survival, but exploration. With every obstacle, they traced the outlines of human destiny.

"Hope drives us," Alyssa said, her voice steady, quietly charged with resolve. "It has carried us through the universe and will continue to do so."

She turned back toward the habitat, her resolve unshaken by the red sands below or the silent vastness above. Hope was their beacon, their anchor, their compass. It would guide them into a new day for humanity on Artoria.

And somewhere beyond that crimson sky, the Horizon waited, patient, immense, and silent, ready to carry them the rest of the way.

Chapter 3

ASHES

When cryopods across the Horizon unsealed, releasing their occupants into wakefulness, the air filled with hisses and the whirring of fans. The sterile glare of the LEDs made Dr. Alyssa Artoria's pupils contract as her eyes opened. Her skin was still cold from the cryogenic mist, a spectral reminder of decades spent traveling through the stars without dreams.

Her limbs felt foreign, muscles aching as she pushed against the pod's casing. Ice seemed to gnaw at her skull, but she pressed a trembling hand to her forehead and forced it away. She gasped in short breaths, tasting the metallic tang of cryofluid and recycled air.

Her voice cracked with disuse. "Status report." At her words, the systems lit up, displaying vitals and diagnostics in clean script.

Others were emerging too, their confusion plain. Murmurs spread as they realized this was no simulation. They had reached the new home of humanity: Artoria. Together, they exhaled a collective breath.

"Dr. Artoria's" focus sharpened. A planet was waiting, and there was work to be done. With the Luna Station insignia as a touchstone, she pulled on her blue research uniform.

With authority born of Luna Station, she declared, "Begin pre-landing checks." Her sharp eyes scanned her team, each member chosen for this moment. "We step onto Artoria prepared and vigilant. Suits on. Equipment check in twenty minutes."

Her movements were precise, a practiced rhythm of calibrations and tests. She checked seals, instruments, and comms. Liora, her daughter, watched with a mix of pride and worry.

"Remember," Alyssa reminded them, "gravity is 1.1 Earth standard. Adjust your movements. Watch for the unforeseen. This is survival, not just exploration."

The team nodded. Scientists, explorers, the forerunners of a new era—they understood the weight of their duty.

"Dr. Artoria," one said, excitement in his tone, "when you're ready, we're ready."

"Then let's make history," she said, staring at the airlock door. She gave one last nod before leading them forward.

Through the viewport, Alyssa gazed at the world below. Sapphire oceans cradled emerald continents. "Look at it," she whispered, awe breaking her composure. "Artoria."

The group pressed closer, faces lit by alien light. The ship's sterile walls felt dull beside the glimmering forests beneath.

"Remarkable," one breathed.

"Stay focused," Alyssa said, though her own heart raced. "We are trailblazers, not tourists."

The landing craft touched down with a tremor. With a sigh, the airlock disengaged.

"First steps are yours, "Dr. Artoria" Liora said, steady.

Alyssa nodded and moved to the hatch. Gravity tugged at her limbs, a reminder that every step here must be relearned. The ground yielded beneath her boots, leaving shallow impressions—humanity's first marks.

"Air is rich," she said, breath visible in the chill. "Gravity is heavy, but manageable. We'll adapt."

Her team followed, each step measured, each motion a vow.

"Begin environmental samples," Alyssa ordered. "We need baselines for water, air, and soil."

"Initial readings are promising," a technician reported. "The biosphere appears compatible. No immediate threats."

"Record everything," Alyssa said. "Every detail matters."

As she stood on Artoria's soil, the scale of their mission pressed in. A world of promise, a world of challenge.

"Let us be careful stewards," she said. "This is our new home, and we must honor it."

Around her, colonists worked with precision to set up life-support and shelters. Yet Alyssa's mind raced ahead—to structure, to governance, to the society that must be built.

"Dr. Artoria," a voice called. She turned to see representatives from the guilds, faces resolute. "Leadership is something we need to discuss."

"Indeed," Alyssa said. They entered the command tent, its walls lit by holographic schematics and data streams.

"Artoria needs a council," the hydro-engineer insisted, hands pressed to the table. "We cannot build this world without unity. Diverse expertise must guide us."

"Agreed," Alyssa answered. "Every voice deserves a platform. The Colonial 9 Council must represent us all—scientists, engineers, physicians, educators."

The farmer added, "Selection should rest on experience and vision. Our future depends on it."

Nods circled the room.

"Then let us hold an assembly," Alyssa said. "The council will be democratic, open, and committed to survival and prosperity. Every colonist will have a voice."

The charge of creation filled the air as the assembly gathered. Proposals, discussions, and votes followed. Individuals with strong credentials and integrity filled the seats one by one.

"Last but not least," a geologist said, her voice echoing through the gathering, "we nominate Liora Artoria to lead this council."

As Liora stepped forward, she glanced at her mother before meeting the hopeful faces turned toward her. She carried herself with seriousness, her confident gait masking the conflict within.

"Thank you," Liora said, her voice steady and clear. "I am honored by your trust. As head of the Colonial 9 Council, I promise to guide our path with diligence and foresight. Our humanity is as important as our survival. We will build a society that not only endures but flourishes through collaboration, creativity, and respect for life."

Cheers rang against the makeshift buildings and spilled into the untamed landscape of Artoria. Dr. Alyssa Artoria, watching her daughter, felt pride and confidence. With Liora's calm direction, they would build something lasting.

"Let us begin," Liora declared, turning to the council. The seeds of a civilization were planted in the unity of these few, but the task was immense.

With her fingers interlaced, Liora sat at the head of the oval table, surveying the Colonial 9 Council. Ideas poured forth, urgency pressed at every face, and the chamber buzzed with low conversation. Sunlight streamed through panoramic windows, gilding the assembly with a golden glow, a reminder of their new beginning.

"Let's call this council to order," Liora said with authority. The commotion hushed. "Our priority is building the framework that guarantees survival and prosperity. Laws, resource distribution, and environmental preservation are the pillars of our future."

Alyssa nodded as her sharp eyes scanned digital documents. Her precise interjections reflected her scientific discipline. "Remember, resources are finite, even though surveys show mineral deposits and water."

Zara Malik tapped her stylus. "Agreed. Our technology helps, but algorithms alone won't balance growth and conservation. We need a full plan for sustainable use."

With a firm tone, Aurek Tyrell added, "Let's focus on that balance. It's not just about surviving—it's about thriving without repeating the mistakes of our past. We fought for this chance."

The council debated earnestly, trading ideas and plans. Applause and nods punctuated talk of recycling, land distribution, and energy sources. Every voice added to the foundation of their civilization, shaping their vision.

Liora summed it up: "Resource management is not a sprint; it's a marathon. Our children's children will walk these lands, breathe this air. Let's make sure they inherit a world where life flourishes. We must think decades ahead, not days."

The members exchanged thoughtful looks. They knew the path would be difficult, but they shared the belief that they were building a legacy meant to last.

Alyssa's eyes returned to the holographic biosphere of Artoria, alive with ecosystems humanity barely understood. As whispers died down, she said, "We stand on the edge of both opportunity and obligation. This planet's biodiversity is not only an asset; it is a responsibility. Our first steps must be taken with reverence for the balance we've observed."

Faces turned toward the projection of iridescent leaves fluttering like soft fireflies in a mock breeze. Tracing routes on the map, one participant noted, "Exploration teams see potential for agriculture here, but if we're careless, we'll damage native ecologies."

"Conservation zones," Liora said firmly. The room held its breath at such restraint in a time of scarcity. "Areas off-limits to development. We'll study them thoroughly before planting a single seed."

"Agreed," another said, "but redundancy matters too. Multiple cultivation biomes could protect us from unexpected pressures."

Alyssa raised her voice. "Which brings us to our next concern." The projection widened, showing the Artorian System with planets circling in arcs. "The settlement of other worlds is within reach."

A generation later, eyes lit with excitement, tempered by the hardships they had faced. Murmurs rippled, expectation colliding with pragmatism. One asked, "We may have the means, but do we have the right to claim these worlds?"

"Rights come with outcomes," Liora answered, her gaze fixed on the planets above. "Strategic expansion could ease Artoria's strain, but we must move slowly and learn here first."

Alyssa allowed herself a flicker of wonder. "Imagine a network of sister colonies, each adapted to its world, each contributing to a shared future."

"Interdependence," someone whispered, the word hanging in the air.

"Only with strict protocols," Liora replied, grounding the moment. "Every colony must mirror our commitment here—environmental studies, sustainable infrastructure, population control."

Alyssa's pride mingled with worry. "Then it's settled. We'll draft permissions and requirements."

The council leaned forward, bound by resolve. Their silent promise was that history would not repeat itself.

Dr. Kellan Ward exhaled, fogging his visor, and tightened the straps of his suit. His team double-checked connections and rehearsed mental checklists as the lander's cabin hummed with energy. Cryostara, a world of endless storms, loomed in the viewport.

“Remember,” Kellan said, steady over the noise, “Cryostara isn’t Artoria. Be ready for anything.”

Cryostara proved him right.

Suddenly, a powerful gust threw the solar array off alignment, causing a flicker in the power grid. “Stabilize it now!” Kellan barked. Within moments, the team secured the array, the lights steadying. With a nod, Kellan pressed on, knowing Cryostara wouldn’t make things easy.

Eyes fixed on the ominous surface of the planet, the crew nodded sharply around Kellan. The lander pitched side to side as gusts battered it, sinking through layers of turbulent atmosphere. Kellan’s knuckles whitened on the armrests, but he held his resolve.

A shudder rippled through their bones as they landed. Under a sky smeared with steely clouds pressing down upon them, the hatch hissed open to reveal a landscape of ochre and russet. Every step reminded them they were on alien ground, the gravity heavier than Artoria’s.

One team member gasped, adjusting her oxygen flow. “Air’s thin. Feels like wading through water.”

Leading across the rough terrain, Kellan ordered, “Keep your breathers on max.” With practiced efficiency, they unfurled habitat modules, structures opening like metal flowers toward the faint sunlight. Bioreactors churned, converting carbon dioxide into oxygen, while solar arrays unfolded and angled themselves.

A scientist scooped up dusty regolith. “Hydroponics won’t like this soil. Hardier strains will have to be engineered.”

Kellan nodded, pride swelling in his chest. To create life on hostile ground was the height of human ingenuity. Cryostara was only the beginning.

Humanity’s reach spread through the Artorian System. Each colony adapted; each settlement endured challenges once thought impossible.

On Seraphina, colonists tapped geothermal vents beneath the ice, glowing cities linked by heated tunnels.

On Ignis, solar farms sprawled across deserts beneath two suns. Water, more precious than gold, was drawn from aquifers and recycled inside biodomes lush with green.

Dr. Alyssa Artoria’s words echoed through every effort—a network of sister colonies bound by restraint and resolve.

On Cryostara, Kellan adjusted his suit’s thermal lining, the fibers tightening against the cold. Rock and ice stretched before him, carved by relentless winds. His breath fogged the visor as crews secured habitats to the frozen ground.

"Keep those heaters running," he commanded over comms. The clang of metal and whir of servos filled the air, reminders that even basic work was punishing here.

His second-in-command, Elara, stood silhouetted against Cryostara's jagged horizon. "Oxygen levels are stable, but we'll need more heat soon."

Kellan watched solar arrays deploy, their surfaces coated to capture what sunlight pierced Cryostara's sky. "Understood. Prioritize the power grid. We can't afford downtime."

From Artoria onward, colonists had mastered adaptation—recycling heat, drawing water through sublimation, turning sparse sunlight into power. Every habitat was a monument to that resourcefulness.

As the sun sank behind a ridge and shadows stretched across camp, Kellan reflected on their tenacity. They had not only survived but flourished, spreading across worlds, each demanding its own form of endurance.

On Sirocco, turbines spun endlessly in sandstorms, feeding power grids.

On Verdant, bioengineers grew crops alongside native flora beneath violet skies, balancing food and ecosystem.

The lessons of Artoria remained central: sustainability, stewardship, progress without exploitation.

“Dr. Ward,” Elara called, pointing toward a ridge where ice met sky. “You should see this.”

Kellan followed her gaze as twilight fell. Auroras rippled along the horizon, ribbons of blue and green twisting in silence.

“Beautiful,” he whispered.

“Beautiful indeed,” Elara agreed. “But we should check the radiation shields. Those auroras mean strong solar activity.”

Kellan smiled. “Always the scientist, Elara.”

Standing atop Horizon’s command tower, Dr. Alyssa Artoria looked out over the dome-covered cityscape of Artoria. Dawn touched the skyline with green and gold. Below, streets bustled with colonists, each step a tribute to resilience. She drew in a breath, tasting the faint sweetness unique to Artoria, her hands resting on the cold railing.

“New worlds, Kael, built from hope and determination,” she whispered.

"Indeed," Kael said, standing beside her, his uniform bright in the morning light. "From here, we see the results of our people—creating life from nothing."

Alyssa nodded, her mind straying to the latest reports from Cryostara, now a shining example of adaptation under Dr. Ward's leadership, and to the growing colonies scattered across the system like gems, each carving its own course while holding to a shared vision. Malik's masterpiece, the shimmering Aegis Shield, arched over their world, catching the rising sun.

"Zara would be proud to see her work alive," Alyssa said, her voice carrying quiet pride.

"Her shields protect us all," Kael replied, "allowing these moments of reflection and growth."

Alyssa glanced down at her communicator, scrolling through messages from Liora detailing the latest Artorian Council decisions. They had guided society through turbulent beginnings with steady leadership, balancing strategy with compassion. The council's dedication was clear—creating laws, overseeing resources, and protecting Artoria's natural beauty.

Alyssa turned to Kael. "Every decision we make, every law we draft, is for those who will walk these paths after us. We are not just surviving; we are thriving, building the foundation for a future full of possibilities."

Kael nodded, his eyes on the vast city below. "Our accomplishments matter—but the true measure will be what future generations do with what we've built."

They watched in silence as the city stirred to life: the rhythm of daily routines, the gleam of technology woven into the landscape, the laughter of children learning in safety. A new era had begun, a civilization born from interstellar struggle yet intent on peace.

"Let's get back to it," Alyssa said with resolve. "There's still much to do."

She took one last look at the horizon before stepping away from the railing, walking toward the day's challenges with Kael at her side. As stewards of a dream built by fortitude, discernment, and the unbreakable human spirit, they carried their roles not as burdens, but as honors.

CHAPTER 4

THE RISE OF RHODOR

With a shriek that cut through the emptiness of space, the first transport ship—a grim monstrosity of iron and rivets—broke through Rhodor's thin atmosphere. Shackles clattered in time with the ship's trembling descent, a clamor of chains that spoke of imprisonment and despair. Prisoners—Earth's cast-off villains—sat shackled in the belly of this metal beast, their steely eyes reflecting the arid landscape unfolding below.

Commander Thorn Valik felt the familiar clench of resolve in his gut as his steel-gray eyes scanned the desolation of Rhodor through a narrow viewport. His hardened soul mirrored the landscape—a canvas of grays and browns where only the strong could survive. His hands—the same hands he believed would one day control the very world now seeking to imprison him—flexed as the restraints bit into his wrists.

The transports landed with a jolt, their pads kicking up dust storms that whirled like wraiths. An oppressive silence fell as the engines slowed—a collective gasp before the prisoners plunged into their new reality. The ship's side creaked open, exposing the bleak silhouette of the automated prison complex beyond. Its sprawling maze of concrete and steel stood as a testament to cold efficiency, silently guarding the desolation. Overhead, drones buzzed, their emotionless surveillance a constant reminder of the system's watchful eye.

At the head of the chain, Valik observed turrets mounted on tall walls, their barrels tracking every movement. Laser grids crisscrossed the perimeter, invisible yet merciless, promising swift retribution to anyone who dared test them. The ground trembled beneath their feet as they neared the facility, machinery humming in perfect unison beneath the surface. Disembodied voices issued commands through concealed speakers—indifferent and absolute—while the prisoners trudged forward. Every step drew them closer to Rhodor's embrace: a world where only survival mattered.

As Valik scanned the facility's entrance, his eyes narrowed. A plan began to form. He knew even the most sophisticated system carried flaws, even one designed to crush the spirit through constant scrutiny. He memorized the layout as he stepped through the doorway into the prison's shadow. These automated jailers would one day learn that not all planets could be forgotten, and not all men could be contained. Valik would rise—and with him, Rhodor.

The arid plains stretched in every direction, scorched by unrelenting heat. Dust-laden winds stung the skin and eyes of the newly arrived, offering neither comfort nor shade. "Keep moving," the automated voice commanded as they were driven toward the work fields. Each prisoner's face carried either grim determination or hollow resignation, manacles clinking with weary steps. Their thin-issue garments offered little protection. Lips cracked and bled; sunburn spread across raw flesh.

Yet among them walked a figure seemingly untouched by the oppression. His eyes remained fixed on the horizon, as if defying the planet itself. His presence carried weight—a silent promise of strength in the face of despair. Shoulders squared against Rhodor's rage, he stood taller than the rest.

Weeks later, during a ration distribution beneath constant drone surveillance, Valik surveyed the crowds. His charisma—his promise of freedom—was the glue holding the disparate factions together. But a different kind of authority was rising in the shadows.

Daeron Kess stood near the perimeter wall, supervising the distribution of nutrient paste to his rapidly growing sub-group. His efficiency was terrifying: his team received their portions, formed a perfect line, and ate in silence, without touching their neighbors or even looking up—a chilling contrast to the chaos and jostling around them.

Whispers followed him like a shadow. Prisoners at nearby stations leaned away as he passed, some muttering prayers, others biting back curses. A few wouldn't even look at him, staring instead at the dust as if eye contact alone might invite punishment. Rumors spread in low, fearful tones: that Kess could stop a man's heart with a thumb; that he slept standing up so he would never be caught vulnerable; that he'd once snapped a drone's neck with his bare hands when it descended too close. Whether any of it was true didn't matter—the fear was truth enough.

A minor dispute flared. A gaunt man tried to snatch a portion from Kess's line. Before Valik could move, Kess's hand shot out. He didn't shout or rage. He simply drove a pressure-point strike into the thief's jaw, knocking him unconscious. Kess then kicked the spilled paste into the dust and stared at the remaining prisoners in his line, his eyes promising the same fate for any sign of greed.

Valik strode over, his voice low and dangerous. "Daeron. You waste valuable resources. The objective is conservation."

Kess turned, his expression utterly blank. "Discipline, Commander, is the most valuable resource. That man compromised the line. Better to lose the paste than invite compromise into the unit." His voice was flat, low, both respectful and dismissive at once.

"You're carving out your own dominion, Daeron," Valik said, steel-gray eyes boring into Kess's. "I lead an army of survivors. You are building a cult of the obedient."

Kess shrugged—a slight, arrogant tilt of the shoulders. "The obedient follow orders. The survivors ask questions. We need the former if we are to take what Artoria claims. When the time comes, the Iron Phoenix—as I call them—will be Rhodor's backbone."

Valik stared at the inert body on the ground. Kess was a viper—useful, but dangerous. "Your methods work. Don't mistake them for command. There is only one leader here."

"Of course, Commander," Kess replied, meeting Valik's gaze with a chilling lack of deference. "But a leader needs a flawless instrument to execute his will. I am simply honing that instrument."

Valik said nothing. He already knew the truth: one day, Kess's ambition would turn on him. When it did, Valik intended to be ready.

As weeks passed, the inmates' survival instincts hardened. Under the watchful eyes of drones that circled like vultures, rations dwindled, water was dispensed with deliberate cruelty, and sleep came in broken fragments. Valik's voice cut through the mutters of discontent. "This place wants to break us," he said, his steel-grey eyes locking onto those who dared meet them. "But we are more than what they say. We survive because we choose to."

The rebellion was already in motion. Valik had planned a precise breach, using localized charges to access the control center without alerting orbital surveillance.

The revolt began under Rhodor's twin moons, one crimson, one ash-grey. The drones didn't detect the first explosion until it was too late. But it wasn't the controlled blast Valik had planned. It was a brutal, overpressurised detonation that tore through the outer wall and deafened men half a field away.

Valik screamed into his comm. "Kess. What in the Void was that? I told you to use a level-two charge."

Kess's voice, filtered by static, was calm. "The perimeter barrier was fluctuating, Commander. A level-two charge carried a high failure probability and risked partial exposure. A level-four charge ensures immediate breach. The objective is achieved."

"The objective was stealth, Daeron. We've just announced our presence to every satellite from here to the Perseus Barrier."

"Then let them watch," Kess countered, his voice flat with defiance. "We are not ghosts, Commander. We are Rhodor. We don't hide our war."

Valik cut the comm. His jaw locked with contained fury. Kess was not only insubordinate. He was dangerously effective, and he knew it.

Valik led from the front, a stolen plasma rifle braced against his shoulder. Daxx Draven was at his side, med-kit repurposed into a field rig strapped across his chest. Alarms screamed as mechanical guards poured from the towers. Red beams sliced through the dust, vaporizing those too slow to duck.

"Push through," Valik roared, his voice carrying over the chaos. "Take the gates."

The prisoners surged forward, an avalanche of flesh against steel. They wielded pipes as spears, torn plating as shields. Sparks rained down as they clashed with drones, the clang of metal and human rage echoing through the canyons. A drone swooped low, cleaving a man apart mid-run.

Daxx lunged forward, tearing a shock baton from the corpse's belt. He jammed it into the drone's sensor cluster. The machine spasmed, shrilling in synthetic overload, before collapsing into the dirt. "That's one," Daxx shouted, eyes wild behind soot-streaked glass.

They advanced under constant fire. Automated batteries rotated with machine precision, spitting red plasma through the haze. Prisoners fell in lines, but others stepped over the bodies and kept moving.

One man, a miner named Rusk, dragged a fallen comrade's oxygen tank into the open. He struck it with a spark rod and didn't look back. The blast shattered the nearest gate.

Valik sprinted through the shockwave, cloak aflame, shoulder bleeding from shrapnel. "Forward," he screamed. "If you stop, you die owned."

As the smoke thinned, one prisoner, eyes wide with fear, glanced toward the advancing Centurions. But it was the sight of Kess and his Iron Phoenix that froze him mid-stride. He ran harder, driven less by the drones behind him than by the knowledge that those elite guards would show no mercy at all.

Inside the compound, chaos gave way to close-quarters brutality. Narrow corridors funneled the attackers into kill zones. Drones hung from the ceilings like spiders, slicing down with methodical precision. Valik dove into a maintenance shaft, the air thick with the smell of scorched oil and burned flesh.

"Daxx," he yelled through the static-filled comm. "On your six."

Daxx burst from the corridor behind him, dragging a wounded guard whose keycard still blinked green. "Found us a ticket."

They used the body's hand to open the blast doors, and a flood of prisoners poured in. Inside, machines turned against their makers. Automated loaders slammed drones into walls, sparks spraying outward like shrapnel.

The corridors were filled with smoke. Men coughed up blood and dust. Somewhere deep inside the prison, power conduits overloaded, throwing violent arcs of electricity across the ceiling. The facility itself began to scream, a chorus of failing systems and dying engines.

At the eastern tower, Valik climbed the wall under turret fire, his boots slipping on molten steel. He reached the platform, wrenched a guard's rifle from its mount, and spun it toward the yard. The plasma cannon belched fire. The gate disintegrated in a roar of white heat.

"That's your god, Rhodor," Valik bellowed. "And we just killed it."

The prisoners below answered with a sound that wasn't a cheer, but a war cry. A single voice of rage and freedom rose above the smoke. By dawn, the sky was black with ash. The automated guards lay in twisted heaps.

Valik and Daxx led the survivors through the breach toward the command spire. Alarms still wailed, though most of the power grid was gone. The two men moved low and fast through the fire-lit corridors.

A drone caught them at the final turn, sleek, new, faster than the rest. It lunged, blades snapping from its arms. Valik went down hard, his weapon skidding across the floor. The drone pinned him, its saw humming inches from his throat.

Daxx didn't hesitate. He leapt, drove a piece of rebar through the machine's eye, and rode the shower of sparks until it fell still.

Valik pushed himself up, panting. "You're insane."

"You're welcome," Daxx said, wiping blood from his cheek.

They reached the core. The air shimmered with heat from overloaded servers. Sparks rained down like burning debris. Valik's hand found the neural cable. With a savage pull, he ripped it free. The hum of oppression stopped.

"Today we claim this place with blood and will," Valik shouted, his voice echoing through the hollow corridors. "Rhodor is ours."

A roar of triumph shook the compound. Prisoners who had been victims embraced one another, now the first architects of something new. Dawn broke across the barren horizon, illuminating not a prison, but the beginning of a society forged by survival.

Weeks later, smoke still curled from the broken towers. The air smelled of oil and ozone. Where drones once patrolled, men now stood guard. Rhodor had no masters, only survivors.

Valik walked the compound perimeter with Daxx Draven beside him.

"You've built an army out of ashes," Daxx said quietly.

"No," Valik replied. "I've built belief."

Their makeshift command tent buzzed with activity, engineers repairing generators, scavengers turning wreckage into machines. Among them was Dr. Soren Alex, the newly self-appointed Chief Scientist and Weapons Engineer. His lab coat was stained with soot and blood, but his eyes gleamed with restless intent.

Valik also noted the growing presence of Kess's private guard. The Iron Phoenix was unmistakable. They wore black, scavenged armor that was identical and polished to a matte finish. They moved silently, never slouching, never speaking to the prisoners. They took orders only from Kess, or through Kess, from Valik.

When Valik entered, Soren stood over a reactor chamber cobbled together from prison machinery and crashed drone cores. The light inside pulsed irregularly, white one second, red the next.

Kess was already there, leaning over Soren, his presence tightening the air around him.

"It's too slow, Doctor," Kess said, his flat voice scraping the silence. "The assembly requires acceleration. We have achieved the objective. Now we must convert victory into leverage."

Soren flinched under the Commander's scrutiny. "It is not a timeline problem, General Kess. It is a stability problem. The containment field is evolving too quickly for the feedback loop. It could breach at any second."

Valik stepped in. “Doctor, tell me about the evolution.”

Soren, relieved, spoke quickly. “We’ve stabilized the main reactor, but it’s changing.” He gestured to a holographic array on the table. Fields of color rippled in slow, hypnotic patterns, overlapping like storm fronts. “We found an anomaly buried in the satellite debris, fragments of Luna Station tech fused with pre-collapse reactor coils. When activated, they create plasma harmonics that should not exist. The field folds on itself, increasing in energy density instead of dispersing.”

Kess cut in, ignoring Valik. “Can it breach Artorian shields?”

Soren nodded, wary. “If we align the plasma vectors through a focused quantum resonance, we can amplify it into a directional energy wave. I call it a Quantum Energy Disruptor, QED for short. It can unmake energy barriers. Any defense field. Planetary or orbital. It does not pierce. It destabilizes. Think of it as hitting a shield with a vibration it cannot resolve until it collapses from the inside.”

Valik’s expression darkened with intrigue. “Can you control the output?”

“Barely,” Soren admitted. He keyed in a command. The reactor hummed, and a tight beam of light lanced upward, a perfect column that flickered between blinding white and blood red. The walls quivered with the frequency. Static crawled across Valik's skin.

"By adjusting the phase frequency," Soren continued, "we can decide how the energy manifests, focused and surgical in white mode, or wide-field devastation in red. It is unstable, but reactive in a way I cannot fully model." The hum deepened into a growl.

Kess stepped forward, his hand reaching for the console. "Then put it in the red cycle. We test it on the next Artorian scouting beacon. Today."

"No," Soren shouted, recoiling. "It needs another seventy-two hours of flux regulation before a field test. It will vaporize itself, and likely us, on output."

Valik slammed his hand down on the console, silencing both of them. "Daeron, sit down. The doctor's timetable is our timetable. I need a usable weapon, not martyrdom."

Kess withdrew his hand slowly, his eyes flashing with raw contempt, not for the risk, but for the delay. "Patience is a luxury Artoria affords itself, Commander. We cannot."

"I decide what we can and cannot afford," Valik said, his voice dropping to a dangerous register. "You built the discipline. I will choose where it falls." He looked at the trembling light inside the chamber. "Shut it down, Doctor."

Soren's hands danced across the console, sweat running into his eyes. The light flared, then snapped into darkness. The room fell silent except for the residual crackle of discharged static.

Valik's voice was calm, almost reverent. "You just showed me a god in a cage, Doctor."

Soren exhaled, shaking. "No. I showed you a storm. And we do not have the cage yet."

Valik approached the viewport, eyes reflecting the faint, dying pulse of the reactor core. "You call it the Quantum Energy Disruptor," he said. "That is a name fit for a scientist. I will give it a soldier's name." He turned, his voice low and steady. "Rhodor's Hammer."

Far across the gulf of space, the moons of Artoria hung serene over the tranquil laboratories of Luna Station II. The hum of the facility was steady, measured, a far cry from the chaos that had birthed Rhodor's Hammer.

Archivist Elen Marik leaned over her console, eyes narrowing at the data feed streaming across her holoscreen. The readouts shimmered with a color she had never seen before, an interference pattern oscillating between pure white and deep crimson.

She frowned. “That cannot be solar activity. It is too rhythmic.”

Her assistant, Arden Voss, drifted closer. “Could be reactor testing from outer sector activity?”

Elen shook her head slowly. “No. The frequency modulation is deliberate. It is not power. It is intent.”

She enhanced the scan, filtering out cosmic noise until the pattern resolved into a pulsing wave. Each cycle built upon the last, energy folding inward, amplifying, as if space itself were under strain.

A tremor rippled through the instruments. Monitors flickered. The air itself seemed to hum.

“What direction?” Arden asked.

Elen’s voice was barely a whisper. “Outer Sector Nine, beyond the Perseus Barrier.”

She adjusted the scope and caught a faint bloom, an expanding halo of ionized light. For an instant, the void itself seemed bruised. Her heart pounded.

“Log this as Event Designation Alpha Nine,” she said. “Cross-reference with all planetary beacons and transmission archives. I want confirmation before I send this to Artoria.”

“Do you think it’s a weapon?” Arden asked.

Elen did not answer. She watched the spectral image fade into static, the crimson afterglow bleeding across the black like a wound that refused to close.

"Whatever it is," she said softly, "someone just whispered in a language the stars were never meant to hear."

She saved the file and stared out the viewport. Beyond the serene arc of Artoria's rings, the faintest shimmer remained, a ghost of red still pulsing, far too steady to be natural.

On the highest platform of the captured command spire, Thorn Valik stood alone. Wind tore at his coat, carrying the acrid scent of iron and ozone. He was savoring the victory, the political weight of his leadership.

Kess approached, his armor clean, his Iron Phoenix already patrolling the perimeter with unnerving precision. He stopped several paces short of Valik, waiting.

"The Iron Phoenix is ready for deployment, sir," Kess stated, bypassing any pleasantries. "We are ready to strike the nearest Artorian outpost. We have the Hammer. Let us use it."

Valik turned, smiling thinly. "We will use it when it hurts them the most, Daeron. Not when your own zeal dictates. You are an excellent hammer, but you must remember that a hammer needs a hand to guide it."

Valik placed a hand on Kess's shoulder, a gesture that was equal parts trust and restraint. "Go. Organize your Phoenix. Secure what remains of the prison. When I am ready to strike, I will tell you the target. Until then, discipline."

Kess nodded, accepting the command with outward obedience, but his eyes, fixed not on Valik's face but on the distant horizon of the Artoria system, burned with a certainty that did not bend.

"Yes, sir," Kess said, his voice flat. He was already measuring the moment when the hand would slip. The pulse of Rhodor's Hammer answered in the distance, a faint red rhythm echoing across the void.

CHAPTER 5

EMPIRE

The chamber of the Artorian Council was still and luminous, its walls of crystal glass casting reflections of the twin suns. Commander Anara Artoria stood before the holographic map of the system her ancestors had helped build—a constellation of peace now bound by fragile alliances. Around her, the council murmured about expansion routes, trade accords, and soil reclamation.

Then the signal came.

It was not on any known frequency, a pulse threaded with distortion and purpose. The voice that broke through was metallic, deep, and unmistakably human.

"This is Leader Thorn Valik of Rhodor. Your experiment in civility ends today."

Gasps rippled through the council. Anara's hand trembled once on the table before she steadied it. "We are explorers, not your enemies," she said. "You escaped your prison world—we do not seek to reclaim you."

Valik's tone sharpened, carrying the cold logic of vengeance.

"You built paradise while we built resolve. You speak of peace while orbiting the bones of our exile. Submit your fleets to Rhodor's authority, or we will make the stars themselves remember our chains."

Anara drew a breath and held it, the moment stretching thin. "Then we will remember you as the last tyrant of the dark."

There was silence. Then a single phrase returned through the static:

"Rhodor's Hammer falls."

The lights in the chamber flickered as the signal spiked. Elen Marik's voice burst over the comm-net from the lunar observatory: "Commander Artoria, the anomaly—it's—" The transmission cut off mid-signal, in a flash so bright it seared through every viewport.

A pillar of light carved through the void, striking Luna Station II, the moon-base that orbited Artoria's sister world. The feed disintegrated into static. When it cleared, there was only a spreading halo of debris—spinning embers where the scientific heart of humanity had been.

No one spoke. The only sound was the faint hum of the power systems struggling to compensate for the electromagnetic shockwave.

Anara pressed one hand against the console, her voice breaking to a whisper meant for no one but history. "So it begins."

She turned to the council. "Evacuate the outer colonies. Prepare the Aegis prototypes. We will defend what remains."

And as the glare faded from the viewport, she saw the scar of Rhodor's first strike drawn across the heavens like a wound that would not heal.

The war room on Artoria erupted into motion. Every console and screen flared with urgent data, tracking fleet movements, energy signatures, and cascading system failures. At the center of it all, Anara Artoria stood rigid, her eyes cutting across the streams of incoming reports. Beside her, General Kael's jaw was clenched in grim resolve, and Captain Veyra Shiran's fingers moved across a holographic interface as she fought to stabilize the command net.

Someone exclaimed, "Another breach!" Anara's heart raced as the words cut through the room like shrapnel. Every breach was more than a tactical failure. It was a family lost, a life erased, a future she had sworn to protect.

Anara said to her staff, "We're fighting blind without the completed Aegis array. Veyra's team is still weeks from planetary integration. Until then, our colonies stand unshielded against the QED."

Veyra said, "Visuals are down," her voice oddly quiet amid the noise. "Our scanners are not picking up Rhodor's cloaking technology."

The weight in Anara's chest hardened. "Estimates?"

Kael replied, "Uncertain, Commander. They've found a way to ghost through our perimeter net," his hand tapping against his thigh.

Anara took a deep breath, feeling the mass of Artoria beneath her feet, a reminder of everything at risk. There was silence for a heartbeat before the battle resumed.

Death rained unseen on the battlefield at Solara, where the sky should have been empty. Soldiers in powered armor darted between barricades and gun nests, their movements frantic, their voices edged with panic.

As though sheer will might repel the unseen attackers, a young private swatted at the air. "Contact! No, false alarm!"

A sergeant yelled, "Stay sharp!" Her gaze swept the horizon, searching for distortion or movement that might betray Rhodor's hidden fleet.

But aside from brief flickers that made hearts seize and weapons twitch, nothing moved. Screams vanished beneath the thunder of an artillery emplacement as it detonated, metal and flame tearing skyward.

With her weapon's targeting system cycling uselessly, another trooper swore, "Dammit, where are they?"

The order came down the line, tight with desperation. "Fire at will! Fire at anything that moves!"

The soldiers obeyed, hurling volleys of plasma into empty air, lighting the atmosphere with streaks of blue-white fire. A few shots struck true, revealing the brief silhouette of a collapsing stealth vessel, a reward for blind defiance.

Rhodor was unrelenting. For every cloaked ship that fell, two more seemed to replace it, their precision overwhelming the Artorians' fractured defense.

Those distant explosions became numbers and symbols on a screen back in the war room. Anara watched them without blinking, searching for patterns that might shift the tide. She knew lives lay behind every fading icon, each loss pressing in silence, but she did not break. She would find a way, for Artoria, for humanity's new home.

On a secondary monitor, a civilian evacuation feed flickered, mothers clutching children, emergency crews herding crowds toward transports beneath a burning sky. A transmission cut through the static. "This is Solara MedBay, patients in transit, systems failing!" The voice dissolved into white noise.

For a moment, Anara's reflection hovered faintly on the screen, layered over the desperate faces of her people. "You'll make it," she whispered, though she knew they could not hear.

Another red blip vanished from the holographic display. Anara's fingers tightened on the console, knuckles whitening. One by one, Solara's defenses, once a constellation of watchful sentinels, were being destroyed.

Her breathing slowed even as her mind raced through probabilities and contingencies. "Options," she demanded, her voice cutting cleanly through the chaos.

An aide replied, his face strained but controlled. "Reinforcements are en route, but they'll arrive too late unless we expose those ships."

Despite the screens showing a colony under siege, Anara remained steady. "Deploy the wide-spectrum flares. Light the sky if you have to." She turned to General Kael, seeking the same resolve she carried. "We needed a countermeasure yesterday, Kael."

Amid the war room's relentless tension, General Kael stood unmoved. His eyes tracked the readouts with cold precision. "Artorian units on Solara, this is General Kael," he said, his voice anchoring the channel. "We're making crossfire zones visible. Regroup at fallback positions Echo and Gamma."

With her gaze shifting between the general and the chaos playing out on her screen, a lieutenant reported, "Sir, our troops are scattered, and visibility is near zero."

With every word carefully weighed and every order cutting through uncertainty, Kael shot back, "Then we adapt. Use thermal barrages, blanket the zones. They rely on cloaking, not invincibility. Echo and Gamma squads, prepare to paint targets for the Skyfire Fleet. I want these ghosts destroyed when their silhouettes register against the heat."

"Understood, General. Coordinating with fleet command now," the lieutenant said, her posture straightening as fear gave way to focus.

Despite the conflict, Anara saw the symmetry of Kael's plan take shape as he orchestrated the defense. A brief spark of pride flared within her, a counterweight to the fear closing in. For every soul on Solara and every hope rooted in Artorian soil, they would stand together. Before the next wave struck, Anara allowed herself a measured breath as the first reports arrived of Rhodor ships caught in the burning lattice of their counterattack.

An island of calm within the storm of war, Captain Veyra Shiran stood amid the clamor of alarms and frantic voices. Her fingers moved with calculated precision across the holographic interface, directing streams of data with practiced control.

Veyra, her eyes fixed on the pulsing readouts, ordered, "Reroute auxiliary power to the sensor arrays. Increase resolution on quantum oscillations. If these stealth ships carry a signature, we will find it."

One of her engineers exclaimed, "Captain, partial matches are appearing on the grid."

"Isolate and enhance those signals. Broadcast the pattern to all units. We are lighting them up like Terran fireflies," she replied, already anticipating Rhodor's next adaptation.

Veyra gave a restrained nod as the first confirmations of cloaked vessels slipping into view crossed the command channel. Solara's fight, however, was far from finished.

Anara stepped beside her, voice low but urgent. "What is this weapon, truly? How does it break shields that should be impenetrable?"

Veyra's gaze flicked across the data. "It is not just energy, Commander. It is frequency. The QED pulses resonate at subatomic levels, destabilizing molecular bonds. It does not matter. It unravels it."

Kael muttered, "They've turned science into a weapon of erasure."

"Exactly," Veyra said. "But every frequency leaves a footprint. If we map the harmonics, we can counter them. We may even feed it false resonance data and collapse its coherence mid-fire."

Anara gave a single nod. "Then find its heartbeat, Captain, and silence it."

Tension thickened the war room. Then a sudden silence fell, heavier than any explosion. Anara's eyes locked on the live feed from Solara as Kael's countermeasures began to shift the balance.

A solemn voice cut through. "Commander, Solara… Solara has fallen."

For a heartbeat, Anara could not breathe. The room tilted, her vision narrowing as if the planet itself had slipped beneath her feet. Then she straightened.

The screen flickered. Solara's defenses lay in ruins, its surface shrouded in smoke and fire.

The loss settled deep. Every dream anchored to Solara had burned away, every life extinguished. Her chest tightened, grief pressing inward.

But Anara did not yield. Resolve hardened beneath the weight of it.

"Assess the damage," she ordered, her voice steady. "I want casualty lists, survivor counts, full status reports."

Her eyes shone with unshed tears, but her gaze did not waver. "We are not broken. Prepare a statement for Artoria. They will know the truth, and they will know we endure."

The room answered with silent nods, grief reshaped into motion by her resolve.

Across the feeds, small acts of defiance played out. Laser rifles and plasma projectors spat fire at looming enemy vessels. Every shot was a refusal to vanish quietly.

Back on Artoria, Anara watched a young soldier drag a wounded comrade to cover.

"General Kael," she said evenly. "No one else dies today. Prepare evacuation shuttles."

"Understood, ma'am," Kael replied.

The war room lights dimmed as power was rerouted to defensive satellites. For a moment, everything slowed. Only the steady hum of reactors and the flicker of failing feeds remained. Anara caught her reflection in the glass, eyes hollow, resolve unbroken. The air carried the scent of ozone and scorched circuitry.

“We hold,” she said softly. “No matter the cost.”

A fresh alert ignited across the screens. Rhodor’s newest weapon, the Planet Grinder, a mobile extension of Rhodor’s Hammer built for sustained planetary destruction, had locked onto Helios.

“Divert all satellites to Helios,” Anara ordered, bracing herself.

The images were catastrophic. A lance of energy tore through Helios’ atmosphere, boiling oceans, collapsing mountain ranges, erasing cities in white fire.

“Cut the feed,” Anara said, her voice barely audible.

The screen went dark. Silence followed, thick and suffocating. It felt as though the room itself mourned. Anara stared at the empty display, sorrow clawing at her chest.

“Status report on all planetary defenses,” she said at last. Loss had forged her resolve into something sharper. “Helios will not fall in vain. General Kael, Captain Veyra, prepare a full strategic assessment.”

Another alert flared. Cryostara, the storm-scoured world at the system’s edge, was under attack.

Captain Veyra spoke evenly. “Rhodor is using the storms. Their ships remain hidden until the final moment, masked by atmospheric chaos.”

“An ambush,” Kael said. “Effective.”

"Adjust tracking algorithms," Anara ordered. "This time, we turn their tactics against them."

On Cryostara, the air screamed like a living force. Lightning split the clouds as soldiers fought knee-deep in mud, redirecting runoff with metal sheets into electrified traps. "Hold the ridge!" someone shouted. A mech fell in flames, its pilot crawling free before rejoining the line with a rifle. Above them, the storm burned with relentless fury.

Back on Artoria, the tension was unbearable. The war room's ceiling lights flickered as data from Cryostara poured in. Kael leaned forward, his voice rough. "Rhodor's adapting again. They've learned to read our heat decoys."

"Then we change the game," Anara replied. "Run the storms through predictive models. Use the lightning to scramble their sensors. Let nature be our ally."

Her team worked frantically, updating projections and recalibrating systems in real time.

The three leaders watched as Artorian forces on Cryostara rallied. Explosions still lit the storms, but fewer ships were being destroyed.

With her voice steady, even as turmoil churned beneath it, Anara asked, "Losses?"

"Decreased by seventeen percent since implementing Veyra's adjustments," Kael answered.

Anara's focus shifted immediately to the next objective. "Good. Keep pressing. We need every advantage we can take. The war is far from over."

Far from the burning colonies, aboard the Rhodor's Will, Leader Thorn Valik watched the holographic feeds dissolve into static. His reflection merged with the red glow of Helios's destruction.

"Three colonies gone," said Daxx Draven, his voice low. "They'll be rebuilding for decades."

Valik did not respond. His gaze remained fixed on the drifting debris field. "Decades are nothing. Let them rebuild. I want them to remember who taught them fear."

Daxx hesitated. "And when they come for us?"

Valik's smile was thin as glass. "Then Rhodor's Hammer will fall again, until their will bends or their worlds break."

The stars beyond the viewport burned in silence, as if bearing witness to the war's first reckoning.

Chapter 6

CRYOSTARA RISING

Kael acknowledged solemnly, his voice barely above a whisper. “Rhodor has anticipated our every move. But we are adapting and learning.”

“Indeed,” Anara replied firmly, though a flicker of unease passed behind her eyes. “It is time we put our people’s resilience to use. We have faced environmental hazards before, but none like this.”

The storm beyond the Cryostara horizon pulsed with blue-white lightning, its radiation casting jagged streaks across the war room glass. Every burst illuminated the trio, Anara, Kael, and Veyra, as if carved from resolve.

Veyra Shiran’s voice was calm but urgent, her eyes fixed on the flood of data streaming across her display. “I have partially compensated for the electromagnetic interference by recalibrating our scanners. It may level the field, but it will not give us perfect clarity.”

“Implement it immediately,” Anara ordered. “And inform the commanders on the ground. Every fragment of information could mean survival.”

The three leaders stood in shifting light as Artorian forces on Cryostara rallied. Despite the chaos, their adaptability showed. Ships wove between thunderheads of plasma fire, and explosions lit the storms like brief suns, yet fewer vessels fell to ambush. They were learning, enduring, evolving.

With her voice steady, even as turmoil pressed beneath it, Anara asked, “Losses?”

“Decreased by seventeen percent since implementing Veyra’s adjustments,” Kael answered, his eyes never leaving the display. His tone was factual, but a trace of relief surfaced.

Anara’s thoughts moved quickly, already mapping contingencies. “Good. Keep pressing. We need every advantage we can take. The war is far from over, even if battles have been lost.”

Veyra’s hand brushed across her console, light reflecting off her lenses. “Agreed. There is more we can attempt. I will continue refining the system. This interference may reveal weaknesses we can exploit.”

Anara inclined her head. “Your expertise saved lives today, Veyra. But we must prepare for what comes next. Rhodor will not relent, and neither will we.”

Kael turned from the hologram, his reflection shifting within the projections. “Strategies for the upcoming engagements?”

“Once Cryostara is secured, we will conduct a full debrief,” Anara said, her voice settling back into command. “For now, stabilize the troops. They are fighting for their lives.”

“Understood, Commander,” Kael replied. There was respect in his tone, an acknowledgment that she had become their anchor.

The hum of consoles filled the air, layered with low communication traffic. Against overwhelming odds, the three stood firm. Together, they would carve a path through the dark, decision by decision.

Her silhouette glowed faintly against the strategic display as she traced Artoria’s border with a gloved fingertip. Each illuminated node pulsed softly, each one representing a life, a family, a fragile future.

“Commander,” Kael said, breaking her focus.

Anara turned. His expression was hard, but beneath it stood faith.

“We always find a way to endure,” he said.

“Indeed,” she answered, her voice quiet and unyielding. “Rhodor may believe they have cornered us, but we will adapt, endure, and prevail, as humanity always has. Survivors, not conquerors, write history."

Her steps echoed as she crossed the room, the metallic floor cold beneath her boots. Officers and analysts looked up from their stations, meeting her gaze as if drawing strength from it. Strategy was already forming in her mind, a lattice of choices and risks bound by resolve.

"Veyra," she called. "Your work today was exceptional. Continue probing their interference algorithms. Find their rhythm before they find ours."

"Without question," Veyra replied, her hands moving across the console with disciplined precision. "My team will not rest."

"Good." Anara stood tall, clasping her hands behind her back. "This is only another night before dawn. Remember, our ancestors reached the stars not merely to exist, but to prevail." Her voice carried through the chamber, and weary heads lifted in quiet resolve. "We have survived dark times before."

A breath of silence followed, and then the subtle stirring of hope, the war room's heartbeat returning.

"Every setback teaches us. Every loss steels our resolve. We are the children of pioneers and warriors. As long as we stand united, no force in the galaxy can break our spirit."

Kael's reply came steady and sure. "Your orders await, Commander."

Anara's lips curved, the faintest echo of a smile. "Then let us begin. We have a destiny to claim and a future to secure."

Light flared across her armor, catching the determination in her gaze. For a moment, she seemed untouchable, an emblem of all that was still possible.

Kael's gaze swept over the recruits at the far end of the command hall. Their eyes met his, a flicker of nerves, then resolve. "Remember," he said, his voice low and resonant, "this is no longer just service. It is survival, for you, for your families, for Artoria."

The words struck like a charge through the room. The young soldiers straightened, gripping their weapons tighter as hesitation burned away.

Kael lingered for a moment, pride held beneath discipline. Then, with a final nod, he turned toward the command deck and disappeared into the hum of machinery.

Across the shipyards, Admiral Veska stood on a raised platform overlooking the skeletons of the Titan-class battleships. The vast hangars pulsed with energy, electric arcs, welders' sparks, and engines roaring within containment fields. The air itself seemed to vibrate with purpose.

Her gaze rested on the half-assembled hull before her. The Skyfire Fleet took shape in her mind, Raptor-class cruisers poised like hunting falcons, Hawk-class interceptors gleaming in their cradles. She imagined them alive in the void, darting and weaving through battle as extensions of her will.

"Admiral," an officer called from below. "AI-assisted navigation protocols are online."

"Run full combat simulations," Veska ordered. Predictive modeling under stress conditions. I want every failure scenario mapped before launch."

She descended the platform slowly, the weight of command pressing on her like gravity. Her reflection slid across the ship's metallic surface, resolute and unyielding. "Perfection," she murmured, "is the only mercy we can afford."

Deep beneath Artoria's surface, Veyra Shiran stood alone amid a symphony of light and sound. The Aegis Shield laboratory functioned like a living system, circuits pulsing, reactors throbbing. Her hands moved across the holographic console with precise control.

"Diagnostic cycle forty-seven A," she said softly. "Initiate QED strike simulation."

A miniature model of Artoria materialized above the console, encased in concentric energy bands. Moments later, an artificial plasma wave struck the hologram with blinding force.

The room trembled as the simulated blast hit. Shields flared, bent, shimmered, and held.

"Analyzing flux," Veyra whispered. Her voice remained steady, though her pulse quickened. "Increase phase variance by two point three percent.

The AI complied, its calm tone cutting through the noise. The barriers flickered, absorbed the next wave, then pulsed outward in a halo of refracted light.

The lab filled with quiet applause as technicians exchanged stunned looks. "Shield integrity nominal," the AI confirmed.

Veyra allowed herself a small, rare smile. "It will hold," she murmured. "For now."

Beyond the reinforced doors, the murmur of gathered citizens grew louder, hope spreading faster than official reports. Artoria, for the first time in years, breathed easier beneath a canopy of light.

Anara Artoria ascended the podium beneath the towering obelisks of Novar's Plaza, a space dedicated to Artoria's original settlers and their vision for the planet. Drone cameras hovered silently overhead. Her people filled the square, faces drawn but resolute.

"Today marks not an end, but a beginning," she declared, her voice carried across the plaza. "We stand united, not only in name or spirit, but in purpose and in action."

Murmurs rippled through the crowd, fear and pride intertwined. She saw mothers holding children, veterans saluting, and workers still in uniform. Their uncertainty mirrored her own, but she set it aside.

"The threat we face is unlike any other," she continued. "The Mandatory Service Act is not a burden. It is a covenant. Every citizen a guardian, every hand a shield. The Rhodorian Empire seeks annihilation. We will answer with unity."

A hush fell. Even the wind seemed to be still.

"We will train together, fight together, and endure together. Unity is our fortress. Every son and daughter of Artoria will rise to defend it."

As her final words faded, the silence broke into applause. It was not loud, but deep, like the first heartbeat of something waking.

Dawn crept across Artoria's training grounds, mist rising from the red soil. General Kael stood before the conscripts, his silhouette sharp against the light. "Again," he shouted.

Boots struck dirt in rhythm. Civilians turned soldiers, teachers, miners, and artists, moved as one. Sweat darkened the soil, feeding the planet that had become both cradle and battlefield.

Among them, a young woman faltered, Kai Loran. Her arms trembled beneath the weight of her rifle. "Up," Sergeant Okeke barked. "You'll thank your pain later."

Kai clenched her jaw and forced her body to comply. She had once been a data analyst. Now she was something else, one of thousands reshaped by necessity.

When the drills ended, the recruits collapsed onto the barracks floor, breath ragged, pride unspoken. In the quiet that followed, Kai stared at the ceiling and whispered, "For Artoria."

Later, in the fortified strategy chamber, Anara stood with her trusted circle, Kael, Veska, and Veyra. The holomap flickered before them, the Rhodorian front stretching across the stars like an open wound.

"Rhodor's QED could shatter our defenses in a single strike," Veyra said. "But if we channel their energy through the Aegis network, dispersion may save us."

Veska folded her arms. "Then our counterstrike must be precise. The Skyfire Fleet's plasma cannons will fire in synchronized bursts. There can be no margin for hesitation."

Kael leaned forward. "Ground units will operate independently, using hit-and-run tactics. Guerrilla formations. We strike, vanish, and bleed them dry."

Anara's eyes reflected the blue of the holomap. "Every piece must move as one. Veyra, how long until full deployment?"

"With full manpower, less than a month."

"Then we proceed," Anara said, each word deliberate. "Every delay costs lives."

"Failure is not an option," Veska murmured. The phrase settled over the room like a vow.

As the meeting adjourned, they filed out in silence, their footsteps echoing in measured rhythm.

Through the heart of Novar, soldiers marched in cadence. Once-lively plazas now echoed with commands and the clang of discipline. Anara watched from a balcony high above, a commander standing guard.

"Commander," Caius said softly beside her. "The air feels different now."

"Indeed," Anara replied, her gaze fixed on the horizon. "I sometimes wonder if we are erasing our past, or forging a new one."

Caius nodded slowly. "You've given them purpose, Anara. Peace was the dream of your ancestors. Survival is the charge of those who came after."

"Survival without identity is hollow," she said quietly. "We came to the stars seeking freedom. Now, to preserve it, we bind every hand to war."

"Perhaps identity," Caius said, "is shaped not by peace, but by what we protect."

Her eyes softened. "Hope," she said simply. "It must remain."

Below, the city thrummed with life and fatigue, a civilization reshaping itself under fire. As she looked down, she saw not soldiers or subjects, but fragments of the dream her ancestors had begun.

When Caius withdrew, Anara remained, her hands gripping the railing. Her voice, barely audible, whispered into the night. "Unity in the face of existential threat."

Above her, the Aegis Shield shimmered faintly against the stars, an aurora of protection. Beneath its glow, Artoria slept, ready to wake to whatever dawn awaited.

Anara turned from the balcony at last. Her reflection lingered in the glass doors, a doubled image. One part human, one part symbol. Both would be required for what lay ahead.

Chapter 7

ICE & IRON

Like a silent statue, Anara Artoria stood at the heart of the Cryostara command center, gazing at the holographic projections that rotated slowly above the console. With each broken transmission, the image depicting Rhodor's troops advancing across the ice plains of Cryostara flickered in and out. She read the silent language of war in the shifting vectors and moving icons, her eyes fixed on the enemy's advance, determination shadowed by fear.

The dome's air carried the brittle tang of recycled oxygen and hot electronics. Heat coils thrummed beneath the floor, but cold still seeped through the seams. The storm pressed ghostly hands against the glass, making the metal ribs creak. Engineers had taped strips of thermal fabric along a hairline crack in the western viewport. Frost still feathered the edge like white breath. Every exhale in the room briefly became visible, condensation flashing and fading within a heartbeat.

“Tactical Commander,” Anara said, her voice level, “we must hold the eastern ridge. Fortify it with everything we have.”

The room’s murmurs stilled. She waited just long enough for each officer to feel the weight of what was coming.

“Cryostara is our bulwark. If it falls, everything else collapses.”

Affirmations rolled back across the pit. Hands moved. Code poured. On the holomap, the ridge brightened in a band of blue, units shifting like beads of light on a string. Someone bumped a console. A cup rattled, the sound indecently loud.

Outside, the wind swallowed sound. Cold gnawed at armor seams and fingers even beneath thermal layers. Soldiers clipped down heaters and cursed as indicators lagged. Mechanics checked the servo torque while steam curled from vents and froze into lace along handrails. A squad jogged past a beacon stake blinking a tired amber. The leader reached out and patted it, as if steadying a living thing.

“Keep those heaters running,” a trooper called. “When frostbite starts to bite back, you’ll wish you fed it earlier.”

"Immortal then," her partner quipped, and the wind tore the laughter away.

Anara listened to their voices, one palm resting on the console. She imagined each as a fragile thread anchored to her by invisible tension. Pull too hard and something would snap. Let go, and everything would fall. She set the thought aside. Leadership was not a metaphor. It was a ledger of lives and probabilities.

A tremor rolled through the ice, a subterranean shiver that lifted dust from conduit housings.

Then the sky opened.

The first Rhodorian salvo came down like a verdict. QED lances carved the storm into violet wounds, melting snow into vapor that refroze midair in glittering sheets. The ground bucked. Energy towers flared, then went dark, their capacitors spent in a blink.

"Brace for impact!"

The dome rang. A seam groaned and held. Anara's screen bloomed with warnings, breach alerts, hull temperature spikes, and external sensor blindness.

"Commander Artoria, we're being torn apart." The voice broke on the last word.

"Divert power to critical systems," Anara said. "Protect infrastructure first. If the spine holds, we stand."

Her hands moved in measured choreography. Subsurface conduits glowed on her display as she rerouted power like blood around a wound.

“Activate the Aegis Shield.”

The command carried across every channel. Deep beneath the ice, pylons unlatched with a hiss and judder that everyone felt in their bones. Field nodes pulsed awake, one, two, twelve, twenty-eight, climbing in a rolling wave beneath the permafrost.

The second QED volley met something that had not existed a breath earlier.

Light struck the curvature and came apart. It fanned across the storm in lambent veils, refracted into harmless brilliance. Where death had fallen moments ago, an aurora walked the air.

“It held. It’s holding. Aegis is holding.”

Relief, raw and disbelieving, broke across the channels. Anara closed her eyes for exactly the length of one inhale.

“Maintain formation,” she said. “No pursuit. Not yet.”

Another strike rolled in. Again, the shield sang with color, and the storm swallowed the sound. Telemetry steadied. The cacophony on the comms resolved from screams into clipped reports.

"Node integrity at ninety-one percent," Veyra said, her voice tight with concentration. Harmonics within predicted variance. We can load more if we must."

"We must," Anara answered. "Reinforce the east. Shift one quarter of output from the west. They are light."

The battle outside slowed, then sharpened. The storm cut both ways. Rhodorian armor coughed and faltered as ice seized gears and vents. Artorian strike teams moved in thin knives of motion, here and gone, firing short, precise bursts. Thermal optics painted enemies as smudged embers behind curtains of snow.

"Delta Squad, north forty meters," Anara said. "Use the glacier lip. Let the drift hide your profile."

"Acknowledged," came Kael's gravel. "Moving with the wind."

Another tremor followed, gentler than the first. Somewhere beyond the dome, a tower collapsed with a deep, bell-like note. The sound reached them as vibration through boots and floorplates.

Anara kept her voice low and even. She had learned from her mother that certainty was contagious. The soldiers called it the Cryostara calm, and they fought better under it.

"Section Nine, rotate arcs. Conserve plasma. No blind fire into the whiteout."

"Copy."

"Med Three, reroute triage away from the east airlock. We are taking shrapnel there."

"Understood. Moving."

On the auxiliary feed, she watched a corridor outside the dome shudder under a blast. Lights failed, then emergency strips flickered to life, painting the walls in pulsing amber. A mechanic lifted a child's drawing from the floor, a shuttle under a blue sky, and tucked it carefully into a tool pouch before running on. Anara's chest tightened, and then she let that pass.

"Commander," Veyra said, "we have a feedback ripple starting at Node Three. It could ladder if it couples with Six."

"How long until it couples?"

"Seconds if we take another full volley on that quadrant."

"Shift phase by two degrees. Bleed load into the western plate."

"That risks meltback."

"Better heat than failure."

"Understood. Shifting."

The next QED stroke hit. The field wavered, flared, and held. On one monitor, hairline cracks spread across a surface layer of ice over a node shaft. Steam rose and crystallized. Veyra's voice returned, ragged with relief. "Ripple damped. Integrity at eighty-six percent and rising."

Across the plain, the Artorians felt it too, the pendulum swing. Squad leaders began to push. The shield was not only a protection. It was courage made visible. Men and women who had been farmers and welders and teachers advanced beneath its glow, jaws set, breath smoking in the air.

"Forward," a squad leader shouted. "For Artoria."

"For Artoria," three dozen voices answered, small in the storm and vast in the net.

In orbit, Admiral Veska's crews rode their own edge of cold, the kind that lurks in vacuum and waits for seals to fail. "Confirm firing window," she said, her eyes on a curve of Rhodorian armor entering a corridor of clearer sky.

"Window in three. Two."

"Fire."

Plasma lances stitched the cloud, clean and white against gray. Below, Rhodorian treads tore and sputtered. A column turned and bogged, drivers choosing snow drift over annihilation. Strike teams hit them like hail.

"Commander," an officer reported, "enemy spearhead buckling."

"Hold formation," Anara said. "We take ground. We do not chase ghosts into the blizzard."

A medic's feed flickered alive on her peripheral display. A man lay on a stretcher, lips blue, an IV line slow as tubing fought the cold. The medic cupped the man's cheek with a gloved hand and leaned close to his visor. "Stay with me. Keep counting. Breathe the numbers. One. Two. Three."

The man blinked, lashes rimed with frost, and breathed.

"Commander," Veyra said, "Aegis reserves at seventy-two percent. At this loading, we can hold at least an hour, longer if Veska keeps breaking their cadence."

"We will not need an hour," Anara said, not as a promise, but as a line.

Another Rhodorian barrage came late and sloppy. It met the shield at the wrong angle and scattered in sheets of harmless color. On the ground, the Rhodorians began to pull back, not with precision, but in fits and starts, as fear took hold all at once.

"Now," Anara said, quieter than before. "Delta Formation. Begin the counter sequence. On my mark."

She raised her hand. Sometimes gesture mattered, even when no one could see it. She held it for three heartbeats as battle groups, wind shear, and cold stress curves aligned in her mind.

"Mark."

Artillery roared. The storm swallowed the sound and turned it into pressure in the gut. Exosuits flared. Strike paths converged into a geometry that, for an instant, resembled a constellation.

"Contact," came a cry, half triumph, half grief.

Through it all, the Aegis field pulsed like a low drum. It did not feel divine to Anara. It felt like mathematics and love forged into something that could hold.

On the far side of the command center, a young officer swayed and braced a hand on the console. Anara placed a palm lightly against the woman's shoulder as she passed, just enough pressure to lend strength, not enough to soften.

"Commander," Kael said, his voice rough, "their line is breaking."

"Secure the ridge," Anara said. "Then the field."

"Copy. Moving."

Minutes stretched. Snow covered the dead quickly. The storm did not distinguish banners. A Rhodorian standard tumbled end over end and lodged against a burned-out vehicle, the cloth freezing into a new shape before it finished falling.

At last, the feeds quieted. No more QED fire struck. The aurora thinned to a pale veil.

"Status," Anara said.

"Enemy in full retreat," came the reply. "They left machines on the field. We are pushing no further. Wounded are being extracted."

The room exhaled, a subtle sound, the sum of many shoulders dropping by a fraction. Someone laughed once, a weak, bright sound. Someone else covered her face and sobbed silently into her gloves for three seconds, then straightened and kept working.

Anara stepped down from the platform and crossed to the auxiliary viewport where the glass was less fogged. The world beyond looked sculpted from light and ash. Torches bobbed. Medics bent like penitent figures. Steam curled from ruptured housings and froze into filaments. The cold had already begun its quiet reclamation, softening the sharp lines of wreckage, frosting edges until even horror looked gentle.

"Commander," a lieutenant said, his uniform scorched along one sleeve, "your strategy saved us."

"We saved ourselves," Anara said. "Remember the cost. Honor it. Bury them well."

She keyed an open channel. Her voice carried across the entire network, intimate and steady.

"You endured," she said. "You fought as one. The shield held because you held. There will be time to tell this story. For now, secure the wounded, mark the fallen, lock down the ridge. Do not squander what you won."

She cut the channel and let the room fill with other voices.

Light years away, Rhodor's command chamber thrummed like a heart in a metal chest. General Daeron Kess stood before a display bleeding red, hands clasped behind his back, hard enough to blanch the knuckles. An aide hovered at the edge of his vision, every muscle arranged into humility.

"Explain," Kess said.

"Sir, the Artorians," the aide began, then stopped, because how did one explain survival?

"A shield," Kess said. "They built a wall against the sky."

"Yes, Commander."

Kess considered. He did not believe in miracles. He believed in miscalculation and leverage.

"Regroup the divisions," he said at last. "Reassign command of the Twelfth. Send two probes to Cygnus. I want schematics before dusk cycle. They have shown us their hand. We will remove the arm that dealt it."

"And the losses, sir?"

"Catalog them. Then build me three new ways to make them irrelevant."

The aide bowed and left with the speed of a man escaping the weather.

Back on the ice, dusk arrived not as color but as pressure in the air, a quiet that thickened and settled into everything left standing. Field lamps rose in cones. The Aegis lattice dimmed to a hum low enough to feel only as a tremble at the edge of perception.

Anara walked the corridor to the outer door. The locks cycled with a sound like held breath released. Cold reached in, intimate, and found the warm places where armor plates overlapped. The first step onto packed snow brought a dry crunch that echoed in the helmet.

She crossed to the ridge where the wind had shaved drifts down to hard surfaces that reflected light like dull metal. From there, the field lay below her in planes and scars. Teams moved along measured lines. A medic knelt with both hands on a soldier's chest and bowed his head for a long moment. Then he rose and moved on.

"Commander," a voice said softly in her ear, careful not to intrude and compelled all the same. "We recovered thirty-two. There are markers for many more."

"See that they are paired. No one lies alone."

"Yes, Commander."

She watched a squad recover a Rhodorian pilot from a shattered frame, moving with the same care they gave their own. The storm had no loyalty. Neither did the ground. Decency was an act of rebellion.

Her mind ticked through lines, resupply, repositioning, a new algorithm for Veyra to test that might damp a different class of spike. Somewhere ahead, diplomacy would have to thread the needle that war had already punched. She allowed that future to exist without stepping into it yet.

"Your names," she said, barely more than breath, "will be etched beside the stars."

The wind took the words and returned them as a whisper that sounded, for the briefest impossible instant, like an answer.

Behind her, the command center's silhouette glowed with work lights where crews already climbed to check seals.

Inside, screens waited for the next pattern, the next surge of red, the next proof that intelligence could be shaped into something that held.

Anara turned, the ridge crunching beneath her boots, her breath a small cloud in a world of larger storms. She felt the weight, not as a burden pressing down, but as a counterbalance that kept her steady. Peace would not be built from victory alone. It would be carved through valleys of loss and held in place by the hands of those who chose, again and again, not to let go.

She descended to the path leading back toward the dome. At the base of the ridge, a young soldier, Elara, stood with her rifle slung, her hands shaking, not from fear but from cold so deep that nerves misfired. She saw Anara and straightened, trying to still them.

"You did well," Anara said.

Elara's breath fogged and broke. "We… we stood."

"You did more than stand," Anara said. "You held."

Elara nodded, her jaw tight, and turned back toward the line of stretchers.

Near the eastern perimeter, Sergeant Okeke barked orders in a voice like iron scraped on stone. "Tighten those anchors. I do not want a single shelter taking wind when this turns ugly again." He glanced up as Anara passed and gave her a brief, precise nod, the kind reserved for truths that endure.

Veyra's voice came softly across a private channel. "The lattice is resting at sixty-four percent. I can tune it to draw less from the grid overnight. It will hum like a heartbeat."

"Let it hum," Anara said. "Let them sleep under it and know they are guarded."

"You did that," Veyra said.

"No," Anara said, and found that, for once, she did not need to say more.

She reached the airlock and paused. Behind her, field lights traced elegant arcs through rising threads of steam. For a moment, she saw the battle as someone else might, months from now, in the clean retelling that turned chaos into story. The day the sky became a wall. The day the cold did not win.

When she stepped inside, warm air wrapped her like a memory of summer and stung her skin. The lock cycled. Seals thudded home. Frost crackled and fell from joints. The corridor smelled of oil and hot plastics, and of the faint human scent that gathers even in the strictest spaces.

She walked back into the command center and onto the platform where the holomap still rotated, gentle now, showing nothing more urgent than terrain and friendly markers. Officers looked up, as if gravity had shifted with her arrival. She nodded, and a quiet steadiness moved through the room.

"Send a message to every sector," she said. "Short. Clear. 'We held. We will hold again.'"

The comm officer swallowed a smile and bent to his board. Keys clicked, soft and sure.

Anara watched the words travel, tiny lights skipping across space, each hop a promise.

She stood very still. Outside, the storm breathed. Inside, the shield hummed. Between those two sounds, she could almost hear the future turning, slow and reluctant, but turning all the same.

And when the next morning found them, they would see them beneath a sky that remembered light.

Chapter 8

THE QUIET WAR

The flagship's command deck held its breath.

Only the low thrum of the central reactor disturbed the silence—a steady bass that vibrated through steel ribs and into the bones of every officer at their station. Frost bloomed and retreated along a hairline seam of the forward bulkhead where coolant conduits ran too close to the ship's skin. Diagnostics scrolled in pale blue columns. The holomap above the dais flickered with a galaxy of icons, some pulsing bright, some guttering to gray. Cryostara's vector still bled like a wound. In the cycles after Cryostara, the war shifted from open battle to silent conflict.

General Kess stood, hands clasped behind him, face composed into something that looked calm and felt like a blade.

"Explain," he said.

The word moved like a pressure wave across the pit. Lieutenant Korin stepped forward, posture exact, mouth suddenly dry.

"Our eastern spearhead collapsed during withdrawal," Korin began. "After the second QED cycle,

Artorian counterfire intensified. Their shield array dispersed—"

General Kess cut him a look. "Adaptation is not a victory condition."

"No, General."

"Then say what you mean."

Korin swallowed. "They out-thought us, sir."

The door behind them hissed. Thorn Valik entered without ceremony: tall, the gray at his temples cut as sharply as his jawline, uniform immaculate save for a fine dusting of carbon along one cuff—a man who still walked his own inspection lines. A few younger officers straightened. Valik had earned his stars on cold rock and thinner chances than this.

"They exploited the ridge geometry," Valik said, voice even. "And our cadence. We hammer, they breathe; we press, they pivot. Aegis made the QED blunt. It wasn't just their shield—it was their timing."

Kess did not turn. "They knew our timing."

"They read it," Valik replied.

Kess faced him now. The holomap swam across his eyes like pale fire. "We publish cadence for a reason: discipline."

"Discipline is not predictability," Valik said. "You've made us easy to read. Their commander understands the space between orders."

A tiny motor somewhere in the ceiling chirred as an optic repositioned. The air itself felt narrower.

"You once met with the Artorian Council," Kess said, the syllables honed. "Before the first mobilizations."

Valik's gaze did not waver. "I was Rhodor's envoy for the ceasefire initiative your office dissolved."

"Was that when you taught them to 'read' us?" Kess asked softly.

A muscle in Valik's cheek flexed. "I taught myself what our enemy valued. It was not a conquest, then."

Kess stepped down from the dais. Up close, his voice softened into something more dangerous. "You remember the mines on Yarrow? The broken air recyclers? The children with metal in their lungs? They remember, too. And you would speak to me of their values."

"I remember everything," Valik said. "Which is why I say this as plain as I can: we are brittle where we should be flexible. You press the same stone until it cracks. Adaptation is strength."

Kess's smile was almost kind. "Strength is obedience made efficient."

"Strength," Valik said, "is a spine that bends before it breaks."

Silence gathered, listening.

Kess inclined his head a fraction, as if the idea intrigued him. "Tell me, General," he murmured, "when you spoke to our enemies, did you tell them what we were?"

Valik did not answer.

"Did you confess our beginning?" Kess asked. "That Rhodor's first flag flew over a penal platform and a list of names? That our fathers were chained in orbit and told to make a world from ash?"

Korin's breath caught. Several officers looked down, pretending focus.

"No," Valik said at last. "Because it is not a confession. It is a history. We remade ourselves."

"And if they have taken that history," Kess said, voice lowering further, "and turned it into a weapon?"

Valik's eyes narrowed. "What have you heard?"

Kess didn't blink. "What I always hear. Everything."

Valik stepped in, closer than decorum allowed. "Then hear this: you are building a prison without bars and calling it unity. You will hold it until it shatters."

"Better a prison built of loyalty," Kess said, "than a republic of doubt."

The reactor throbbed. The command chronometer ticked over with a hollow click.

Valik's voice dropped to something only a few could hear. "You are losing them, Daeron. Not because we fell at Cryostara. But because you cannot imagine a world that doesn't answer to you."

He turned. The door sighed open; cold air licked the threshold. As Valik stepped through, Kess's voice—almost gentle—followed him.

"Security," he said. "Surveillance on Thorn Valik. Full spectrum. Discretion."

A light above the aft console blinked a compliant green.

General Kess mounted the dais again. On the map, the Cryostara vector pulsed, then faded. He breathed in, measured, as if taking the ship's temperature through the soles of his boots.

"Proceed," he told Korin, and the room exhaled like lungs finally allowed air.

The rumor started as a whisper in a maintenance subnet that never should have seen the light of day.

A technician, bored and angry, cracked a checksum because it felt good to pry something open. A line of text unfurled from a packet marked ROUTINE: CALIBRATION and sat like a coiled thing inside a diagnostics pane.

RHODOR WAS BORN IN CHAINS.

He almost deleted it. Instead, he captured the packet, stripped its tags, and sent it along with a shrug emoji to a cousin in a barracks two levels down.

By the second shift, the message had replicated across ghost channels—old soldier group threads no one had bothered to archive because letting them die felt like sacrilege. By the third, the phrase had jumped into unaudited proximity syncs—screens lighting up when two devices lingered too long near the same rail.

In Barracks K, Sergeant Brask watched six displays bloom in eerie synchrony. The same three lines appeared in stark text on every screen, the font system-default, bland as an invoice:

PRE-COLONIAL ARCHIVE EXTRACT

TRANSPORT DESIGNATION: RHODOR—PENAL CONSORTIUM

STATUS: EXPENDABLE LABOR

“Turn that off,” Brask snapped, even as he found himself reading it again. His thumb hovered over the kill switch and did not press.

Across from him, Corporal Rani held her pad like a fragile thing. “They wouldn’t… archive something like this if it weren’t—”

“Propaganda,” Brask said, too fast. “They seeded our nets. You think the Artorians can’t fake a header?”

A veteran in the corner—gray at the temples, a thin scar running down one ear where a comm implant had been ripped out and reinstalled twice—breathed through his nose. “Propaganda doesn’t smell like the air in the ore lifts,” he said. “Doesn’t make your teeth ache with memory.”

“Shut it,” Brask growled. He looked to the door as if the thought itself might walk in under arrest.

In Habitation 7, a vendor froze mid-transaction, loaves of processed grain held out to a mother with a tired child. The vendor’s payment slate lit: the same lines, then a link, then a spool of clipped images—documents with creases scanned into them, the language stilted and old, an Earth seal no one alive had ever touched.

The mother’s lips moved. “Expendable?” she whispered. Her child reached for the bread and, when she did not notice, for her hand.

In a corridor, auditors walked past with neutral faces and lenses that recorded everything. A maintenance pair leaned against a service ladder as if on break, palms to the rail, eyes downcast. One of them—Joren—murmured, “Control, not honor.”

His partner flinched and elbowed him. “Walls have ears,” she hissed. “Kess listens.”

“Good,” Joren said, so quietly that only he heard his own courage. “Let him.”

The message metastasized. Someone overlaid it on a training sim’s skybox, so that recruits running obstacle courses looked up and saw RHODOR WAS BORN IN CHAINS drifting like a cloud. Someone else threaded it into a morning devotional chime: the word chains ringing soft as a bowl.

Light-years away, Artoria’s strategy chamber was the opposite of Rhodor’s: no windowless bunker, but a high, vaulted room whose dim, coffered ceiling held soft light like a kept dawn. Cold vapor from air scrubbers feathered a faint halo near one corner. Banks of holos cast pale geometry across polished stone.

Anara Artoria stood at the central table, one palm flat against a glassy interface, the other curled around a cooling cup of tea she’d forgotten to drink. The dryness on her tongue said the tea had steeped too long; the heat against her skin said she kept it anyway.

“Initial telemetry indicates uptake across three sectors,” said Seyi, her signals chief, voice quiet. “Our carriers reached the Fleet channels and the mid-level municipal nets. Civilian loops are already rebroadcasting through proximity pings. It’s viral.”

A second advisor—Caius, older, unblinking—tilted his head. “Their auditors will adapt. They will clamp down. You designed this to relapse. That is… elegant.”

Anara’s eyes remained on the model. Two constellations pulsed: one pale, one red. Between them, filaments—some broken, some taut.

“We’ve handed them a weapon they can turn inward,” she said. Her voice was steady, the words close-packed. “We must manage the collapse we’ve started.”

A younger officer, eager, could not help himself. “Or we press the advantage,” he said. “We can seed the broadcast layers with imagery that—”

“We are not executioners,” Caius said mildly, which in his language meant be quiet.

The young man flushed.

Seyi cleared her throat. “Commander, donors on the northern farms asked whether we’d consider opening our channels for civilian testimony from Rhodor, if it comes. They want to show… common ground.”

"We show nothing," Anara said. The words landed like stones set with care. "We watch. We learn. If the structure buckles too fast, people are crushed beneath it. We did not fracture an empire so we could inherit a famine."

She flexed her hand off the interface. A faint smear of condensation there matched her palm. She stared at it as if it were a map of something only she could see.

"Peace," she said finally, more to herself than to the room, "is a path through other people's ruins. If we walk it, we carry the weight."

She set the tea down and did not drink. "No further transmissions for now. Monitor. And flag any signal that looks like a purge order."

Seyi nodded. "Understood."

Anara turned her face toward the viewport. Beyond the layered shields of Artoria, the stars looked colder than they had the night before.

Every empire dies of the stories it tells itself, she thought, not saying it aloud. *We have merely hastened theirs. Make sure we do not drown in the echo.*

Korin stood in a lift alone and watched the door seams breathe. Each floor the lift crossed hummed through his boots as a dull bass line. He could hear his heart in the pauses. He could also hear a voice from years ago—his own—pledging an oath in a training hall that smelled of solvent and iron.

Serve the chain that became a banner.

Valik had pinned the insignia to his collar himself. After the ceremony, Valik had spoken not of glory but of temper. *Metal hardens best when you ease it from the fire,* he had said. *Or it becomes glass and breaks in your hand.*

Korin had not understood at the time why a general would speak of easing and not of victory. He understood now. The chain had been drawn too tight around the neck of a nation. You could hear the crack in its links if you were quiet enough.

The lift sighed open to a maintenance corridor that smelled like cold oil. Pipes ran overhead like ribs. A red service light blinked slow, slow, slow.

Valik was there, as promised, half-shadowed by an access ladder.

"You were followed?" Valik asked.

Korin shook his head. "Security's busy pulling old cams from Barracks K. The rumor spread faster than their procedures."

Valik's mouth flattened in something that might have been humor on a different world. "Procedures break at the speed of fear."

They stood for a second with the old loyalty between them bright and dangerous.

"We can't draft policy in a corridor," Korin said finally, voice low. "But we can make a promise."

"To whom?" Valik asked.

"To Rhodor," Korin managed. He tasted the name and found ash in it.

Valik's gaze softened by the smallest fraction. "I did not come to this lightly," he said. "I believed in him. He believed in Rhodor. But belief turned inward becomes worship. Worship answers no one."

"Kess will call it treason," Korin said.

"He already has," Valik replied. "We will call it a correction. History will call it something else, and nobody will agree."

"I want to believe we can do this without blood."

"Then plan for blood," Valik said. "It is the only way to have fewer bodies to count."

Korin exhaled. The air tasted like metal. He held out his forearm.

Valik gripped it. The old oath burned through the leather of their gloves like heat.

"For Rhodor's survival," Valik said.

"For Rhodor's survival," Korin answered, and heard in his own voice the sound of something breaking and something else taking its shape.

They let go. Footsteps clacked at the far bend. Valik melted into a service alcove and was gone. Korin became motion—just another officer in a corridor, head down, duty in every line of him.

On the civilian levels, the rumor went from script to incantation.

A schoolteacher—Mera, forty, shoulders permanently rounded by years of leaning over desks—stood before a class of ten-year-olds while the lesson slate glowed faintly with the words she had been told never to speak. She turned the slate off, then back on, then off again. The children watched her face instead of the screen because children know when an adult is on a ledge.

"What does it mean?" a boy asked, voice invisibly small.

Mera looked at the map of Rhodor tacked to the wall—lines of transport routes and mine clusters and the stylized phoenix that the Ministry required every classroom to hang. She had taught them that the phoenix was resilience. She had not taught them that it was a bird we invented to make ourselves feel better about fires we set.

“It means,” she said, choosing the slowest words she had, “that where you begin is not what you have to be.”

That night, she deleted her lesson plans and wrote new ones around a kitchen table while the lights dimmed to energy-saver mode and the heater clicked twice and failed to come back on.

In a factory, line workers did not speak the words aloud, but their hands faltered in unison on the third shift, and no one shouted at them for it. In the markets, transactions went through more slowly because people stared at each other too long. In devotions, voices wobbled on the lines that used to be sung without thinking.

A city is a machine. The proof that its engine is failing shows up first in the small gears.

By the fourth shift, security nets threw up auto-flags every time the phrase RHODOR WAS BORN IN CHAINS appeared in any public channel. By the fifth, officers were ordered to scroll through private threads. By the sixth, those officers began to pretend they had scrolled when they had not.

On the seventh, a small unit on the southern rim received an order to arrest a medic who had forwarded a scan from an archive. The unit’s captain looked at the name and closed the message. "We didn't see this," he said. Nobody argued.

Artoria's strategy room lived in a hush that wasn't silence so much as focus, wearing a coat. The air smelled faintly of ionization and old paper. Someone had left a scarf looped over the back of a chair; Anara noticed such human things and was always a little surprised by them.

"Commander," Seyi said, voice pitched not to carry beyond the table. "Two new clusters: Dockside in their capital and Sector Eight in the southern mines. Both civic. Both rebroadcasting without comment."

"Any sign of a counter-message?" Anara asked.

"Not yet. We're seeing scrubbing orders—blanket removals, ban lists, account freezes. But no narrative answer."

"They can't answer without admitting it exists," Caius said. "That's the trap."

"Traps catch animals," Anara said. "People just find other doors.

A junior analyst at the end of the table cleared her throat. "Permission to speak, Commander?"

Anara nodded.

"I worked on famine models," the analyst said, eyes flicking between Seyi and Caius, as if asking them to be the grown-ups she was trying to be. "If unrest spreads to their distribution centers, food and med dispersal will lag. That's where the deaths stack. If we keep pressure on their nets, we could—" She stopped herself. "My point is: there's a threshold where collapse isn't just their problem."

Anara listened all the way through, which is rarer than agreement. "What's your threshold?" she asked.

"Forty-eight hours of disruption in more than three hubs."

"Flag me at twenty-four," Anara said. "And draft aid protocols that don't look like aid."

Seyi blinked. "You want to help them feed their cities."

"I want children not to starve because we were clever," Anara said, the steel in her voice not pointed at anyone present. "Design cover: weather anomalies, anonymous donors, a ship with faulty transponders nobody wants to chase."

Caius smiled just enough to count. "You plan to smuggle bread into an empire that will kill us if they catch us," he said, tone like warmed stone. "It appears the Commander remains herself."

"Only on good days," Anara said. She reached for the tea and remembered she didn't want it, and set it down again.

Outside the viewport, Artoria's shield flared and dimmed as a patrol passed, the membrane of a lung breathing.

General Kess did not convene a council. He preferred corridors when the ship slept.

He walked them without escort, pacing himself on the lights that came alive row by row as if the flagship expected him. His gloved fingers drifted along the cold seam where a wall panel met a pillar, feeling the faint vibration of the reactor two decks down. He had always loved that hum. It meant the machine trusted him enough to tell him how it was doing.

He stopped at a memorial wall etched with names added after Cryostara. On Yarrow, memorials were listed on ration slips. On Rhodor's ships, they kept one polished plate for every engagement because the Ministry had learned that polished grief is easier to sell.

He touched a name: a pilot he had trained himself. "They believed," he said, not sure whether the words were praise or indictment.

Around the corner, a night tech froze, not expecting a commander to walk where techs walked. Kess nodded to him as if they were equals and kept on.

At a junction, he leaned toward a camera dome and said, conversationally, "Security."

A tone chirped. “Commander.”

“Internal order,” Kess said. “Codename Purity. Quiet. You will identify any officer whose first loyalty is to a narrative not issued by this deck.”

A small pause, as if the ship itself thought. “Parameters?”

“Begin with Thorn Valik’s sphere. Then Korin’s. Expand as needed.”

Another pause. “And when identified?”

Kess watched his breath fog the lens and vanish. “Fear,” he said softly, “is a poor teacher. But it educates quickly.”

He resumed walking. He passed a viewport where stars were thick and a distant gas giant blew a ribbon of storm off its limb like a tear. He did not look.

Back in the command chamber, he isolated a cluster of signals, dragging them with two fingers into a clean pane. Valik’s region. Intercepted fragments nested like shells. He read the first line of one, then another, then another, until the words blurred into a texture and the texture into a conclusion.

“Ancestors of criminals,” he said, the phrase finally leaving his mouth like acid.

His reflection in the console looked older than the man who had stood there a week before. He disliked the thought.

He straightened, squared his shoulders so the reflection would behave, and keyed a route directly to the disciplinary corps.

“Let them whisper,” he said to the empty room. “Let them question.”

Lights along the ceiling flared and settled as the ship took breath again.

“I’ll remind them who we are.”

Rhodor reminded people of who they were by taking things away.

By the tenth shift, the first food line lengthened because administrators spent their morning checking comm threads for banned phrases and forgot to open the dispensary on time. By the twelfth, a triage clinic in Sector Six went dark for forty minutes because a medic had been flagged and his replacements argued in the hall over whether the flag mattered. By the fourteenth, a transport arrived without three crates of antibiotics because a loader saw the message on a foreman’s screen and stared at it for two minutes, and the crate lifecycle timed out and was rerouted to audit storage.

None of it looked like a collapse. It looked like small pauses that would not add up if you did not count.

General Kess's order began to move through the spine of the machine. Purity did not look like soldiers at the doors. It looked like a changed password. It looked like a superior asking a subordinate to repeat the oath with the line about "source of command" emphasized. It looked like a closed-door commendation followed by reassignment to a post no one could find on the map.

Valik watched from inside his own circle as data streams he had walked across for years slowed under him like a river gone to sand. He adjusted his routes. He sent a message to a friend in Logistics who sent back only a single punctuation mark and then nothing at all. He did not try again. He moved three officers he trusted into positions that looked like demotions and felt like lifelines. He set a time. He did not set a date.

Korin went home to a metal-walled apartment, took off his boots, and sat with his feet on cold tile to remind himself that he had a body. When the wall screen lit with the phrase again—RHODOR WAS BORN IN CHAINS—he did not turn it off. He stared until his eyes watered, then wiped them and made a list of names—people he would not sacrifice unless there was no other way.

On the other side of the stars, Anara slept for an hour in a chair at the edge of the strategy table, chin tipped toward her shoulder, a crease on her cheek from a seam in the upholstery, the weight of command slumped the way weight slumps when a back stops holding it for a second. Caius draped the forgotten scarf over the back of the chair and dimmed the room to a twilight that had never existed on Artoria's surface but felt right here.

When she woke, she did not start. She looked at the model again and then away and then back, as if staring at a bright thing long enough would teach her how not to be blinded by it. Seyi placed a report cube in her hand and did not speak. Anara pressed her thumb to it. It unfolded light into the shape of updates and thresholds and an alert that read: THREE HUBS AT RISK.

She closed the cube.

"Begin the quiet deliveries," she said. "Make them look like mistakes."

Seyi nodded. "Yes, Commander."

Anara touched the rim of her cold cup, anchored by that small circle. "And Seyi—pull the second phase of the transmissions. If we can slow the story, we should."

Seyi hesitated. "It diminishes pressure."

"It diminishes casualties," Anara said. "We are not here to watch people starve."

Seyi's face, a study in professionalism, softened. "Understood."

Anara lifted her gaze to the viewport. A patrol's ion wake made a pale scar on the shield membrane, then faded as the field knitted itself whole.

On Rhodor, General Kess returned to the memorial wall in the morning cycle and found a single faint fingerprint smudge where his glove had touched the metal the night before. He wiped it with his sleeve until the plate shone. He did not like the idea that a mark could outlast the motion that made it.

A junior officer entered, eyes forward, spine exactly the length the Ministry preferred. "General. Incident in Dockside: crowd disruption at food distribution. Dispersed without injury."

Kess nodded. "The word?"

"Contained," the officer lied, not even to please. To survive.

"And Valik?"

"Comms normal," the officer said, which meant scrambled and rerouted and strange.

Kess dismissed him and stood a long while longer watching his own ship breathe.

He keyed one more order into the quiet.

"Prepare tribunal protocols," he said. "Seal them. Trigger on my authorization alone."

He did not say a name in the line. He didn't need to.

In a room on Artoria, Anara listened to a recording: a child's voice asking his mother if he was descended from criminals. The mother's answer was a sound, not a word. Anara stopped the recording before the sound could finish. She set the device down and pressed her fingers to her eyes until stars burst purple behind her lids.

"We've cracked the empire," she said to the room, to herself, and to Caius, who had returned and stood near enough to hear and far enough to be kind. "Now keep it from bleeding out on us."

Caius grunted assent. It was the sound he made when he agreed with her heart.

"Send a message to every sector," Anara added, voice finding its armor again. "No gloating. No commentary. One line."

Seyi waited, stylus hovering.

Anara looked through the viewport at a sky that had learned to bend around them and said, "Tell them: Hold your positions. We do not mistake a fracture for a fall."

Seyi nodded. "Sent."

Anara closed her eyes for a breath, then opened them onto the day she had chosen.

General Kess's last act of the cycle was to stand alone in the command chamber and narrow the holomap to a single icon—the node that corresponded to Valik's reserve. He watched it pulse, steady as a heart under a palm.

"Let them whisper," he said again, and the ship pretended not to listen.

He zoomed the icon larger until it filled his view and blurred, a bright disk without edges.

"I'll remind them," he whispered, "who we are."

Lights along the ceiling brightened to waking as the ship turned its face toward a star no one on board would ever touch. The Quiet War had found its shape. It would not stay quiet long.

Chapter 9

THE PURGE

The dawn above Velskar looked bruised. Smoke from the upper foundries stained the sky a dull, hemorrhaging crimson, as if the city itself were bleeding into the atmosphere. The air, thick and heavy, carried the metallic tang of hot iron and the sharp, sterile bite of ozone. Below, the streets that once hummed with the chaotic symphony of traders, clattering machinery, and workers' shouts had emptied overnight. Shutters were bolted with a new, desperate finality. Lights were dimmed behind grimy transparisteel, leaving the avenues to the gloom.

The first sign of the purge wasn't the siren—it was the silence. A deep, unnatural quiet fell like a shroud, broken only by the whisper of wind through empty market stalls.

Then came the Seekers.

They moved in phalanx formation through the main concourse, their armored boots striking the steel-plated avenues in a single, percussive rhythm more machine than man. Their armor was black chrome, polished to a liquid gleam that reflected the pallid, sickly morning light. Their faceplates were utterly blank, anonymous, except for the faint, pulsating red glow of their visors, scanning, always scanning. Above them, dagger-shaped drones floated, trailing banners bearing the twin suns of Rhodor—a symbol that now felt less like a standard and more like a brand.

Overhead, the loudspeakers crackled to life with a sound like breaking bones. The voice that poured from them was female, mechanically modulated, impossibly calm.

"This is the Voice of Order. All citizens will remain indoors. Loyalty evaluations are in progress. Failure to comply will be treated as an admission of guilt."

Her voice repeated, a cold, digital litany echoing through the cavernous alleys, through the hollowed-out markets, through the fortified courtyards of what had once been a prison and was now merely pretending not to be one.

In the industrial quarter, a mother yanked her child back from a window as the Seekers passed. The boy's small, trembling voice whispered into the stifling air, "Are they coming for the bad people, Mama?"

She didn't answer, her own breath held, her hand clamped over his mouth not in anger, but in a primal need for silence, her heart hammering a frantic counter-rhythm to the Seekers' marching beat.

Lieutenant Korin stood rigid at the perimeter checkpoint outside the central sector, the air shimmering with heat from the newly erected thermal shields. The cloying smell of engine oil and the sharp, sour scent of human fear clung to the cold walls. Around him, soldiers moved like automatons, their eyes downcast, avoiding each other's gaze. In a purge, everyone looked guilty; a stray glance could be construed as a conspiracy.

"Unit Sigma—proceed to loyalty assessment," an overseer barked, his voice stripped of all inflection.

Korin saluted automatically, the motion practiced and hollow. The badge on his chest blinked a sterile blue for clearance, but the guard watching him lingered a heartbeat too long, his eyes boring into Korin's before the wave of a gloved hand granted passage. That moment of hesitation was a verdict in itself.

He passed a long line of detainees forced to kneel beside the soot-stained wall—officers, engineers, clerks, their faces a mosaic of defiance, terror, and numb acceptance. Their wrists were bound with pulse-restraints, glowing bands of energy that hummed and tightened visibly when a detainee's heart rate spiked. A Seeker moved down the line, its movements fluid and efficient, scanning each person with a thin, invasive beam of light across the iris.

One man, a logistics officer, Korin recognized, flinched. His pulse-restraint flared bright orange and constricted violently. He choked, collapsing forward onto the grimy floor, gasping for air that wouldn't come. No one in line looked away, but no one spoke either. The silence was a heavier punishment than the shock.

Inside the command compound, the intercom droned again, the words seeping into the metal and into the mind:

"Order is obedience. Obedience is loyalty. Loyalty is life."

The message played on a loop, its rhythm inescapable, a cognitive prison.

Korin moved deeper into the labyrinthine corridors where the walls hummed with hidden machinery, the sound a constant, low-level threat. Each of his steps echoed against the hollow metal, a lonely sound in the oppressive stillness. He could still hear last night's illicit broadcasts echoing in his head—the frantic whispers revealing Rhodor's origins, the shocking truth that their glorious empire had begun as a galactic penal colony. The truth had spread faster than fire through dry tinder, and the fear of that truth had followed faster still.

He turned a corner and froze.

Two Seekers were dragging away an officer he knew—Captain Relna, a sharp-minded strategist from his own unit. Her face was a bloodless mask, her uniform torn at the shoulder. Her voice was a raw, hoarse scrape. “Korin, for pity’s sake, tell them—!”

One of the Seekers, without a word, struck her across the mouth with a crackling shock baton. The impact cracked through the corridor. Sparks snapped in the charged air, the scent of ozone and burnt flesh briefly overwhelming. Korin flinched, his jaw locking so tight his teeth ached, but he said nothing. He stood, a statue of complicity. In that moment, even silence felt like the deepest form of treason.

When she was gone, the corridor was emptier for her absence, and he kept walking. His mind, screaming in the quiet, whispered a terrible realization: This isn’t just a purge. It’s an erasure. Of her. Of the past. Of us.

Citadel Velskar’s bones remembered their original purpose. It had once been a central prison block, its massive, vault-like corridors lined with cell doors still welded shut from the inside, silent testaments to forgotten inmates. Now, it served as the cold, beating heart of Rhodor’s command.

Daxx Draven walked through the central hall with measured calm, his heavy boots striking the worn stone floor with slow, deliberate notes. He knew what awaited him beyond the towering, engraved tribunal doors. Still, his spine remained straight, his gaze forward. He did not flinch. He thought of his wife, waiting on the farm he’d never see again.

Outside the chamber, Seekers stood in two silent, mirror-polished lines. Their armor reflected his approaching form, a dozen distorted images of a man walking to his end. As he approached, they turned their blank visors in unnerving unison. The air was thick with the acrid scent of sterilizing chemicals, a smell that failed to mask the underlying odor of cold stone and fear.

Draven paused, just for a moment. A thousand thoughts crossed his mind—the first war he had fought as a young lieutenant under Valik's command, the grim day General Kess seized power in a bloodless coup that had since grown anything but, the oath he had sworn to serve truth and the people before any single man. He had broken none of them, and yet here he was, branded a traitor for honoring them.

The massive doors slid open with a hiss of pressurized air.

Inside, the Warden's Chamber glowed with a hellish, pulsating red. Ancient prison lights, never meant for comfort, pulsed through a haze of chemical vapor, bathing everything in the color of fresh blood and old rust. Rows of officers knelt along the edges of the floor, their uniforms stripped of insignia, their identities scrubbed away.

At the center of the room, standing before the empty Warden's throne, stood General Kess. His expression was carved from ice, his eyes chips of flint.

"General Draven," he said softly, the quiet tone somehow carrying over the thrum of the chamber. "Do you know why you stand before me?"

Draven's voice was worn but steady, like river stone. "Because you fear ghosts more than you fear your enemies."

Kess's eyebrow rose a fraction. "Ghosts?"

"The past, Kess," Draven said, his gaze unwavering. "The truth you're trying to bury under a mountain of forced obedience."

Kess descended from the dais, his boots echoing in the cavernous space like a death knell. "Truth doesn't matter to the dead."

"Then you'll have plenty of company where you're sending me," Draven replied, a faint, weary smile touching his lips.

A humorless, razor-thin smile flickered at Kess's mouth. He made a subtle, almost dismissive gesture.

Two Seekers stepped forward from the shadows. Panels in the floor lit up, and shimmering energy fields activated around Draven's body, caging him in light. His breath caught—not in a gasp, but in a final, controlled sigh—

as the light enveloped him, rising from the floor in a column of pure, white-hot flame. For a single, searing instant, his outline glowed, etched against the red haze like a saint in a forgotten icon. Then he was gone—not ash, not smoke, but simply unmade in a silent surge of annihilating light.

Kess turned slowly to face the assembled, kneeling officers, his face a mask of cold triumph. For the briefest moment, his fist clenched behind his back, as if to remind himself the illusion must hold.

"Let this be our renewal," he said, his voice low but penetrating every corner of the silent chamber. "Rhodor is not, and never was, a colony of criminals. We are the architects of our own destiny. And I am the living proof."

As if on cue, the Voice of Order came alive over the speakers, its calm tone a stark contrast to the violence just witnessed:

"Citizens of Rhodor, remain calm. Justice preserves us. Treachery will be cleansed."

Outside, a crowd had gathered, their faces upturned toward the glowing thermal plumes rising from the citadel's roof—the only funeral pyre a hero like Draven would get. Some prayed silently, their lips moving soundlessly. Others just watched, their eyes wide with a trauma that would not fade. None dared to speak the questions burning in their minds.

The purge spread faster than smoke on the wind.

Across the lower districts, the once-mighty factories—the engines of Rhodor's power—had been perverted into makeshift holding zones and execution grounds. The bright banners of loyalty fluttered mockingly beside newly constructed gallows and smoldering firing pits. Sirens wailed a constant, mournful dirge from the watchtowers. Drones hovered, their red scanning beams like malevolent eyes, probing windows for any flicker of movement, any sign of life.

Rumor, that last desperate currency of the oppressed, said the old Foundry Quarter had become the final refuge for those who would not kneel.

There, in the deep, perpetual shadow of rusting blast furnaces and silent conveyor belts, Korin walked alone. His uniform was smeared with ash and grime, the colors of Rhodor muted under the filth. Overhead, armored airships moved with a slow, predatory grace, like carrion birds circling a dying beast. Somewhere far off, the distinctive, low-frequency hum of the Seekers' engines permeated the air—a sound more felt in the teeth and bones than heard, a sickly pulse beneath the city's skin.

He stopped at the jagged mouth of a collapsed drainage tunnel, drawn by a faint, furtive flicker of light within the darkness.

"Don't move," came a voice, ragged but firm, from the blackness.

From the shadows, a figure resolved itself. It was Valik.

He was almost unrecognizable—thinned to a gaunt silhouette, his face hollowed by exhaustion and pain. One arm was wrapped in a blood-crusted sling. His once-immaculate uniform was torn and filthy, the emblem of Rhodor crudely scraped away, leaving a raw, frayed patch on his breast.

"Korin," Valik said, his voice a dry rasp. "I thought Kess would send his dogs for me. Not one of my own."

"I don't know what I am anymore, sir," Korin answered, the truth of the admission hanging bare between them.

Valik's chapped lips cracked into a faint, grim smile. "Then you're already halfway to being free."

He reached into his tattered coat with his good arm and withdrew a small data crystal shard. Its core glowed with a steady, warm amber light, a tiny beacon of defiance in the gloom.

"These are the original records," Valik said. "The convict manifests. Every name, every ship, every crime that brought our so-called noble ancestors to this rock. General Kess ordered them all destroyed. I made… copies."

Korin stared at the shard, a thing of immense, dangerous power. "If he learns you're alive—if he even suspects—"

"He will," Valik interrupted, his voice gaining a sudden, fierce strength. "That's the point. A man can hunt a shadow. It's harder when the shadow turns and stares back."

Above them, the sound of engines shifted, growing louder, more focused. The ground began to tremble with their imminent approach. Time was up.

Valik stepped forward and pressed the warm crystal into Korin's palm, closing the younger man's fingers around it in a firm, final grip. "Keep it safe. The truth is the most powerful weapon we have, but it needs a survivor to wield it. Not a martyr."

The glow of the shard reflected in the wide, terrified whites of Korin's eyes. "Where will you go?"

"Nowhere," Valik said, and with a final, resolute look, he stepped back into the consuming shadows of the tunnel. "History needs its martyrs, Korin. Now run."

The Seekers descended from the smoke-choked sky like a swarm, their black, angular wings slicing through the haze. A blinding, actinic light filled the tunnel mouth, followed by a deafening roar as the explosion ripped through the old foundry. The shockwave struck Korin like a physical blow, throwing him backward across the gritty steel floor. Heat washed over him.

When his vision cleared, his ears ringing, he rose on unsteady legs. Where the tunnel had been, there was nothing left but a crater of molten slag and raging fire.

He clutched the data shard to his chest, its hard edges digging into his palm—a tiny, burning coal of truth in a world of lies—and turned, disappearing into the falling ash and the gathering night.

High above Artoria's orbit, the flagship Aegis Prime hung in the void, a silent, polished blade against a field of stars. Inside, Anara Artoria stood alone at the expansive observation deck, her own pale, determined reflection floating ghost-like against the sea of diamond-bright suns and swirling nebulae.

Her aide, a young man with a face yet unlined by war, approached softly, holding a glowing holopad. "Intercepted transmissions from the Rhodor core, Commander. It's chaos. Purges. Public executions. Entire cities under martial lockdown." He swallowed, the sound loud in the quiet. "Leader Valik is presumed dead."

Anara didn't look away from the stars, her hands clasped tightly behind her back. "And Kess?"

"He's consolidating control with brutal efficiency. The main fleet is grounded, locked down by loyalty officers. All civilian channels have gone silent. It's… quiet."

"Then he's blind," Anara said, a cold certainty in her voice. She finally turned, her eyes meeting those gathered behind her. "And when a predator closes its eyes to devour its own," she let the sentence hang for a beat, "that is when we strike."

She faced the star-flecked glass once more, her voice dropping to a soft, controlled whisper. "Prepare the fleet. Target their outer supply arteries—the depots at Cygnus, the fuel silos at Veridia. No grand assaults. Precise cuts. While Rhodor devours itself from the inside, we sever its veins. Minimize civilian harm. We strike only what feeds their war machine."

Outside the viewport, the distant ships of the Artorian fleet began to shift formation. One by one, their engines flared to life, burning a fierce blue against the black.

Faint and distorted, the Voice of Order echoed from the holopad on the floor, a ghost from a world tearing itself apart:

"Rhodor endures through silence."

Anara's lips curved into a thin, hard smile. She whispered her answer to the stars, a promise and a threat.

"Then we will speak louder."

And the fleet began to move.

Chapter 10

ASHFALL

The command bridge of the Dominator was a tomb, washed in the pulse of red alert lights. Every display screamed a litany of failure—casualty reports from the outer sectors, refinery moons gone dark, and a vital fuel relay fractured, spilling volatiles into the void. Six thousand Rhodorian dead. Six thousand names that would be added to the pyre of General Daeron Kess's pride.

He stood before the main viewport, a statue of imposed calm, hands clasped behind his back so tightly that the leather of his gloves strained. His eyes, chips of flint, were locked on the slow, crawling data stream that marked not just a military defeat, but a profound humiliation. The Artorians hadn't just struck; they had executed a clinic in asymmetric warfare, proving ghosts could outmaneuver his vaunted fleet.

No one dared speak. The only sounds were the low, urgent chimes of incoming damage reports and the strained breathing of the crew. The air recyclers, struggling with a faint leak from a conduit, filled the space with the scent of ozone, coolant, and cold metal—fear given form.

"Who authorized the strike?" Kess asked, his voice so quiet it seemed to absorb the ambient noise of the bridge.

A junior officer, his face pale, swallowed audibly. "It was a coordinated assault, sir. No single command signature. Surgical. Precision drones hit the depots simultaneously. They were in and out before our point-defense could achieve a target lock."

"Precision," Kess repeated, tasting the word like poison. He turned from the screen, the reflected crimson glow hardening the lines of his face into a mask of grim fury. "A coward's word for a stab in the back. If Artoria wishes to test strength, they will learn what strength truly means."

His gaze swept the bridge, lingering for a moment on the empty seat beside him. General Kyra Valis's station was a stark void. Her name was being systematically erased from records even as he stood there, her image purged from databases, her commendations incinerated. Treachery, he knew, required memory to be burned first.

Later, in the austere silence of his ready room, Kess stared at the only physical remnant of Kyra Valis: a single, forgotten data slate containing a treatise on counterinsurgency tactics she had written at the Academy. He had read it a dozen times, searching for the flaw, the first hint of ideological rot that would lead her to betray the

Rhodorian Imperium for the so-called “enlightened pragmatism” of Artoria.

"To understand an enemy's strength," her words glowed on the screen, *"one must first appreciate the source of their cohesion. Shatter that, and the body will follow."*

He had thought her brilliant. Now he saw only the arrogance of a philosopher who believed she could control the chaos she unleashed. Her “precision” had been a message, a taunt aimed directly at him. She knew his mind, his doctrines, his reliance on overwhelming force. And she had exploited it, proving his fleet a lumbering giant, blind to the scalpels already cutting its tendons.

A chime sounded at his door. “Enter.”

His intelligence officer, a gaunt man named Vrolik, stepped inside. “The traitor’s network is deeper than we feared, Commander. The drone signatures were masked by a cascade failure in our IFF protocols—a failure initiated from within. She had help in Engineering and Logistics.”

Kess didn’t look up from the slate. “Root them out. All of them. Public tribunals. Let the fleet see the cost of disloyalty.”

“And the… response?” Vrolik ventured carefully.

Kess finally lifted his gaze. “The response will be absolute.”

In the ship's forward observation bay, Kess stood alone, watching his fleet align for the kill. Gunmetal hulls, scarred and proud, caught the harsh light of Rhodor's twin suns, becoming a thousand gleaming knives waiting to fall. His own reflection in the reinforced transparisteel looked less human than the warships—a thing sculpted from rage and vacuum, a monument to a cause that had long since curdled into obsession.

"They think truth is a weapon," he murmured to his ghostly double, the words swallowed by the silence. "A noble strike for a noble cause. Let's show them that lies can kill just as efficiently. That chaos is a more lasting lesson than principle."

The first volley launched in a disciplined, horrifying sequence. Columns of pure energy, brighter than any star, arced away from the battleships and into the void, their terrible beauty disappearing into the fathomless dark toward the faint, peaceful glimmer of Verdoria. The Dominator trembled—not violently, but with a deep, resonant shudder—as the recoil of unimaginable power rolled through her colossal frame. On the bridge, crew members exchanged wordless, wide-eyed looks. None spoke of civilians, of families, of the moral abyss they had just hurtled into. None dared.

As the firing sequence locked in for its second, cataclysmic salvo, a young comms officer, barely more than a cadet, stood from her station. Her face was a mask of tear-streaked terror. “Commander… sir. The initial scans… Verdoria’s planetary shields are nonexistent. Their orbital defense platforms are outdated, meant for meteor deflection. This isn’t a military target. It’s… It’s a slaughter.”

The silence on the bridge became absolute. Every eye, wide with a mixture of fear and a desperate, shameful hope, turned from the girl to the Commander.

Kess turned slowly, his expression not one of anger, but of cold, clinical assessment, as if she were a malfunctioning circuit. “Officer Jyn,” he said, her name a soft indictment. “Your emotional assessment is noted—and irrelevant. This is a lesson in scale. They killed six thousand of our soldiers. We will erase one of their worlds. The math of deterrence is brutally simple.” He nodded to the security detail by the door. “Escort Officer Jyn to the brig. Charge her with insubordination in the face of the enemy.”

As she was led away, sobbing, the last fragile resistance on the bridge broke. The crew bent to their tasks with a grim, mechanical efficiency. Kess didn’t watch the tactical feed. He had no interest in the real-time data of annihilation. Instead, he stared into the absolute darkness between the stars and imagined the silence breaking—not with screams, but with the simple, physical reality of a world ending.

Verdoria's dawn began in quiet color, a soft lavender and gold bleeding across the horizon. The planet, a jewel of green continents and azure seas, hung in the silence of its orbit, oblivious.

Inside Orbital Outpost Helion, Technician Lira Vehl sipped her bitter synthetic coffee and watched the world turn below. She was on the final leg of a double shift, her eyes gritty with fatigue. Her console hummed, a steady, reassuring presence. Taped beside the primary display was a small, slightly faded photograph—her eight-year-old daughter, Kaelen, standing before the shimmering bioluminescent rivers of Artoria, her smile a beacon across the light-years. Lira traced the image with a calloused finger, a faint, weary smile touching her lips. Two more weeks. Two more weeks and this posting would be over. She'd promised Kaelen a trip to the crystalline shores of Lake Meridian. The thought was a warm ember in her chest.

The outpost's comms officer, a lanky man named Elrin, swiveled in his chair. "Picking up a massive energy spike from the outer marker. Beyond anything I've ever seen. It's… It's reading like a fleet emergence, but the signature is all wrong. It's too concentrated."

Lira frowned, her technician's mind snapping fully awake. "A drill? A new Artorian engine test?"

Before Elrin could answer, his panel erupted in a scream of static and light. "Gods… multiple contacts. Rhodorian warship signatures. They're… they're powering weapons. Lira, they're targeting the planet!"

The console flickered. A single, jarring glitch in the stream of green status lights. Once. Then twice.

The omnipresent hum of the station's reactor stuttered, choked, and died.

A faint tremor rolled through the deck plates—not a violent shake, but a deep, resonant thrum that traveled up through the soles of her boots and into her bones, like the breath of something colossal awakening in the void. The main lights dimmed to a dull emergency amber. Her coffee cup quivered, sending a single, perfect ripple across the dark surface before it slid from the console and shattered against the floor.

Lira's training kicked in. System failure. Core breach. She turned from her station, her heart hammering against her ribs, her eyes searching the viewport for the cause.

The stars were gone.

Where the constellation of the Serpent should have been, there was only an expanding wall of blinding, actinic white. It was soundless—a light that devoured everything. It wasn't a weapon; it was a new sun being born on their doorstep. Elrin was screaming something into the dead comms, a warning that would never be heard. For a fraction of a second, she saw the intricate lattice of the station's outer gantries begin to glow, then twist, then vaporize.

The viewport imploded. The pressure of her life, the air from her lungs, vanished in an instant. The last thing Lira Vehl's mind registered was not the searing heat or the tearing metal, but the small photograph of her daughter, torn from its tape, spinning weightless and serene toward the burning, roiling clouds of the world below.

The light of Verdoria's death, traveling at the universe's speed limit, would take eight minutes to reach the eyes of those on Artoria. Eight minutes of ignorant, devastating peace before the knowing.

On Artoria, the air in the High Council chamber of Novar was thick and still, dimmed to the cold glow of emergency lighting. Through the panoramic armored windows, smoke from distant industrial fires, ignited by

Rhodorian sabotage, painted the horizon a bruised, angry red.

Anara Artoria stood before the central holo-table, a solitary figure surrounded by her silent, ashen-faced advisors. The report hung in the air between them, its cold blue text seeming to leach the warmth from the room.

VERDORIA DESTROYED. ORBITAL SATURATION EVENT.

LOSS OF LIFE: EST. 2.3 MILLION.

TRANSMISSION ENDS.

No one breathed. The number hung in the air, too vast to comprehend. It was not a statistic; it was a black hole, swallowing all sound, all hope, all precedent.

Anara's hands tightened against the table's polished edge, her knuckles white. The veins along her wrists stood out, pulsing with a contained, seismic fury. But when her voice came, it was preternaturally calm, a blade sheathed in ice.

"He answered our precision with extinction."

Her chief aide, a man named Evander, found his voice, though it was cracked and thin. "Madam, the colonies are in panic. The newsfeeds are… It's chaos. Refugee vessels are already overloading the orbital docks, scrambling to leave the inner systems. We can't possibly—"

"Let them move," she interrupted, her gaze never leaving the holo-report. "Do not impede the civilian exodus. But our priority is not control. It is compassion. Redirect all nonessential military assets. Send the medical fleets—the humanitarian corvettes—first. We stabilize who we can. We save who is left to save."

Anara turned from the table and walked to the great window. Below, the capital city of Novar stretched out, a testament to centuries of Artorian peace and progress. Spires of graceful alloy reached for the sky, interwoven with greenways and public art. Soon, the first waves of shock and grief would hit the population. The panic Evander feared would become a tsunami.

An older councilor, Garvin, a man who had served her father, spoke softly. "Anara, we must sue for peace. Now. Before he turns that fleet on Artoria itself. We cannot win a war of annihilation."

"This is not a war anymore, Garvin," Anara said, her back to him, watching the city. "It is an extermination. A peace negotiated with a man who commits genocide is not peace. It is a delayed surrender. He will not stop until our culture is ash and our people are a footnote in Rhodorian history." She finally turned, her face illuminated by the distant fires. "Kyra Valis warned us he was capable of this.

We chose not to believe her. That error in judgment has cost us a world."

She looked directly at her fleet commander. "Activate the Horizon battlegroup. Recall the Whisper and her sisters from the dark. Their orders are to strike only when unseen, to bleed his supply lines, and to vanish before he can retaliate."

Evander hesitated, his moral compass reeling. "A full counteroffensive, Commander? Without a declaration? The Senate… the people… they will call it a dishonorable war."

"This is not a counteroffensive," Anara answered, her voice dropping to a whisper that carried to every corner of the silent chamber. "This is a reckoning. There will be no broadcasts. No triumphant proclamations. Only precision—and silence. We will make his empire rot from the inside out. We will use the shadows Kyra taught us to wield."

Outside the high windows, the familiar star-line of the galaxy shimmered faintly through the planet's thin haze. But now, something new drifted down across the great capital dome—fine, gray flakes, settling over the manicured gardens, the gleaming monuments, the roofs of the sleeping city. Ash, borne on the solar winds from the funeral pyre of a world. From a distance, it might have looked beautiful, a gentle, silent snow. But every flake, every single one, carried the condensed memory of Verdoria, of Lira Vehl, of two million three hundred thousand souls.

Anara closed her eyes for a single heartbeat, the weight of the dead pressing down on her. She thought of the promise of peace, the eight-minute lag that had once felt like an inconvenience in interstellar communication, now a sacred, terrible buffer between innocence and damnation.

"Eight minutes," she whispered, a raw confession of grief for the peace she had lost, for the peace her people would never know again. "That's how long it lasted."

Then she opened them again, and all that was soft was gone, replaced by a resolve as hard and cold as deep-space iron. The woman who valued truth and precision was buried alongside Verdoria, and in her place stood a leader forged in the fires of a new, darker age.

"Prepare the fleet."

The first flakes drifted down just after the second dusk cycle, spiraling lazily through the shafts of golden streetlight that lined the upper terraces of Novar. Children pointed upward, laughing, chasing the powder as it settled over their sleeves. Snow was a rarity on Artoria, a meteorological novelty spoken of in storybooks.

Jalen Rhyse stepped out onto the balcony of his modest high-rise flat, pulling his work jacket tighter around his shoulders. He'd been repairing transit relays for sixteen hours straight after the sabotage strikes, and his bones ached with the familiar exhaustion of a man who could no longer afford fear.

He held out a hand. A single gray fleck landed on his palm, melting into a smear of soot.

Not snow.

A soft breeze carried more down across the city, settling on rooftops, gardens, and market awnings. From the promenade below came confused murmurs that slowly smothered the children's laughter. The flakes were too fine, too uniform. They fell without cold. They tasted metallic in the air.

A woman near the avenue gasped. "It's coming from the orbital streams—look!"

Jalen lifted his eyes. The great sky-shield, normally invisible, shimmered with a faint auroral ripple as particulate matter danced against its curvature, glowing softly in the planetary lights.

A news-drone buzzed overhead, projecting a neutral advisory tone. "Air quality fluctuation detected. Citizens advised to remain indoors until atmospheric regulators confirm particulate composition."

But Jalen had worked in the orbital yards as a young man. He had seen the ash that drifted from ship-recycling furnaces, from old war-scrap incinerators. He knew the signature. Knew the dead-gravity fall of it.

His stomach twisted.

This wasn't from a reactor leak.

This wasn't industrial.

This was… too much. Too widespread. Too fine.

His neighbor, old Marrek from the end of the hall, stepped out beside him, clutching the railing with trembling hands. "You feel that?" he whispered. "Like—like grief in the air."

A message alert chimed from inside Jalen's flat. He turned slowly.

Three words pulsed on his holo-screen:

EMERGENCY BROADCAST PENDING

The ash continued to fall, soft and silent, coating the city like mourning cloth. And Jalen knew—before the broadcast, before the officials spoke, before the truth became a wound the whole world would carry—that something unimaginable had happened. Something vast.

Something that had turned a distant sun into dust.

He brushed a final flake from his hand. It left a gray streak across his skin.

He did not wipe it away.

Chapter 11

SHADOW FLEET

The bank fell into a tense, stunned silence as the screens flickered and died. At first, customers tapped at unresponsive terminals with the usual irritation reserved for technical hiccups. But the silence stretched, seconds turning into uneasy minutes. Then came the realization.

The accounts were frozen. No credits. Novar's digital lifeblood had clotted in an instant.

A woman at the counter broke first. "Please, I just need to buy medicine for my son! It's for his nutrient shunt—it has to be purchased daily!"

Another man barked, "Can't you do something? Anything? My quarterly settlement was due this hour!"

Their voices rose not in panic, but in desperate disbelief—the sound of a society that trusted its systems too deeply to imagine failure. Outside, lines lengthened around corners, citizens spilling into the streets as a hollow dread worked its way across Novar. In every district, screens glowed with error codes or black emptiness, cold mirrors reflecting fear that gripped each heart like a vise.

The damage traveled fast, moving from finance to infrastructure.

In the outer manufacturing rings, towering assembly lines froze mid-motion. Operators shouted over blaring alarms as robotic arms stopped inches from collision. Nothing responded. The core industrial sectors, the city's muscle, were instantly paralyzed.

Transit hubs stalled into sprawling webs of gridlock. Elevated skimmers were locked in place on magnetic rails. Lights flashed static red. The silence from the transit system was almost louder than the chaos—the sound of millions of journeys ending simultaneously. Thousands abandoned their skimmers and crowded the walkways, shouting questions nobody could answer.

A mother clutching her son shoved through the mass, her face pale.

"Is the water still working? Did the pumps shut down? I have nothing stored!"

Nobody knew. The network failure meant critical infrastructure status was a complete unknown.

Rumors leapt like wildfire, twisting fear into paranoia.

"It's Rhodor! They've hacked the Aegis Shield!"

"No—it's internal sabotage! A move by the Council to seize power!"

"We're under attack! A real one, not a skirmish!"

"This is a collapse!"

Two merchants nearly came to blows arguing over blame near a jammed credit terminal, drawing a frightened crowd around them. And above all this, the fear deepened, turning citizens against each other.

Commander Anara Artoria stood before a wall of monitors streaming fragmented updates from across the city. The initial shock had passed from her face; now only cold resolve remained.

"Status updates," she ordered, her voice cutting through the rising noise.

Lieutenant Sienna's fingers flew across a holographic console, her expression tight. "Power grids are holding for now, routed through manual substations. Transportation is down entirely. Emergency services are being rerouted manually, but response times are doubling."

Another officer chimed in. "Medical facilities are mostly isolated from the main network. They're safe from the hack, but communication is breaking down across multiple sectors. They're running blind."

"Restore food and water supply chains first," Anara said, pacing. "We can't let panic take root. It's more destructive than any virus."

Sienna hesitated. "Commander, the chatter is overwhelming. There's… definite talk of Rhodorian involvement. They're calling it Operation Soft-Glove."

"Speculation won't help us," she answered firmly, though the name lingered like a shadow. "Focus on stabilizing the essentials. Send emergency teams. Every minute counts."

All around her, the command center throbbed with frantic energy—officers shouting updates, flickering screens, pages of code streaming past like bleeding data. Anara felt the pressure of a million lives resting on her ability to make sense of the noise.

The crisis was not just a failure; it was a deliberate obfuscation. Anara's top coders, Captain Veyra's core team, were hitting layer after layer of impenetrable digital noise.

Chief Analyst Joric, a man who lived and breathed network architecture, slammed his fist on his desk. "It's impossible! The routing tables are fractal! Every time we trace the initial intrusion signature, it forks into a billion dead ends. It's like chasing a shadow through a cloud of static."

Anara walked over, looking at the incomprehensible, beautiful mess of the core Artorian network on his console. “Is any data recoverable? What did they do to the credit structure?”

“They didn’t steal funds, Commander,” Joric whispered, fear in his eyes. “They didn’t crash it. They just replaced the entire ledger with an empty, immutable block. It’s not broken; it’s gone. And they left a single, high-level cipher—it’s like a mocking signature—protecting the new block.”

“Rhodorian?”

“Worse. It uses the old Pre-Sovereignty encryption protocols. No one has used this tech in two hundred years. It was tailored, Commander. They knew exactly where to hide it.”

Anara stared at the screen. A tailored key, hidden in deep history. This was not a random attack. This was precise, patient, and terrifyingly well-informed.

At Starlight Medical Center, backup generators buzzed weakly, their fuel consumption rate now the most critical data point in the city. Nurses hurried between patients whose lives depended on machines barely clinging to power.

Dr. Lira Han wiped sweat from her brow. “Keep critical-care units routed to the isolated consoles. If power dips, we ventilate manually. Assign two nurses per terminal.”

A young nurse, Lira Han’s niece, stammered, “Doctor, what if the fuel runs out? We have forty-seven life-support cases.”

Han cut her off gently. “Every minute we keep them alive buys the Commander more time. Focus. Don’t look outside—look at the monitor in front of you. That is your universe right now.”

Outside, citizens pressed against the flimsy barriers, dozens pleading for medicine and triage. Inside, the air tasted like fear and stale oxygen. The medical staff was fighting a war of inches against the city’s collapse.

Chaos erupted across Novar. Civilians pounded on bank shutters. Screens stared back blankly. A grocery depot emptied in minutes as security vanished. Riots sparked over dwindling supplies of processed protein.

“Back in line!” a security officer shouted, his voice cracking. He stood rigid in armor, but panic glinted in his eyes.

A fight broke out near a ration dispenser. An elderly man fell and was nearly trampled.

From a command-vehicle feed, Anara watched the tactical screens. Her heart clenched, but her expression stayed steel-hard.

"Status," she demanded.

"Looting in several districts, Commander," Sienna replied grimly. "Forces are stretched thin. We are losing control of District 4."

"Deploy reserves to medical centers and food hubs. Civilian safety first."

Her gaze landed on the tactical feed from District 4—specifically on a young family caught in the surge: Kai, the father, shielding his wife Kael and their daughter Tali from a desperate, surging crowd. A security guard, mistaking Kai's protective stance for aggression in the dim light, struck him with the butt of his riot stick. Tali screamed, a high, raw sound that cut through the command center's low hum, even on the heavily filtered audio.

Anara's fist clenched hard enough to leave crescent marks in her palm. "Zoom in. Send peacekeepers to that sector. Now. Prioritize de-escalation."

"Commander, we're diverting critical assets from the infrastructure hubs—"

"That's an order, Lieutenant! We do not abandon our people. We do not become the enemy!"

Because every citizen mattered, and if the government lost the trust of its people, Rhodor had already won.

Minutes later, Anara faced the Council in a dim strategy room glowing with floating maps, her adrenaline still spiking from the image of Tali's scream.

"Rhodor's appetite for destabilization is no secret," she said, her voice sharp with accusation. "We must consider that they orchestrated this as a political tactic."

General Hahn frowned, clutching his datapad. "But Commander, our firewalls—Veyra's system is state-of-the-art."

"Never underestimate them," Anara said, stepping into the center of the room. "They tailored this. I want an investigation. Immediate, deep, and without political interference."

Senator Tyrell, calm and impeccably dressed, leaned forward, a predator scenting weakness. "Are you suggesting an inside job, Commander Artoria? Are you prepared to name the traitors in this room responsible for your own technological failures?"

"Until we prove otherwise, everything is on the table, Senator," Anara shot back, holding his gaze. "The enemy's goal is to turn us against each other. Your rhetoric in the plaza suggests you are eager to help them."

General Hahn cleared his throat, trying to regain control. "Enhanced interrogation? We must find the source."

"No," Anara said instantly, her resolve unwavering. "We do not become what we fight. We use logic and data. But time is our enemy. Move fast. Trust no one until cleared."

Tyrell steepled his fingers, a small, knowing smile playing on his lips. "A noble, if naive, stance, Commander. But the people need a clear enemy, and they need a strong hand to clean up the mess your administration has overseen." In the flicker of his eyes, it wasn't just power—it was the thrill of watching order unravel. "They are looking for a new leader, Anara. One who can speak to their fear, not hide behind code." The implication was a heavy, cold weight.

In the central plaza, Senator Aurek Tyrell's words, broadcast via unauthorized portable uplinks, were still echoing. The crowd, buzzing with fear, had quieted as he raised a hand.

"Friends, neighbors, Artorian citizens," he began, voice smooth as polished stone. "We stand on the edge of collapse, betrayed by the very systems we were promised would protect us!"

The crowd stiffened. He continued, letting the accusation hang in the toxic air.

"Stores are empty. Credits are frozen. Our infrastructure is in disarray—all under the leadership we trusted! Ask yourselves: Why did our most sensitive security fail so spectacularly and so fast?"

A murmur surged through the masses, morphing from fear into dangerous, actionable anger.

Tyrell paced, his voice rising to a calculated roar. "We need strength, not excuses! Action, not promises! I vow to restore order. No enemy—not even Rhodor—will dare strike us when I lead!"

Thunderous cheers met his words, a wave of populist fervor that bypassed the command structure entirely. And a subtle, dangerous rebellion bloomed, sponsored by the very crisis it claimed to solve.

Back in the command center, flickering screens illuminated Anara's face, tracing the lines of exhaustion and mounting fear. Her fingers hovered over the last fragments of corrupted code that Joric had managed to isolate.

"Rhodor's signature is all over this," she murmured, more to herself than to Sienna.

She saw the patterns, the tailored nature of the attack, but the bigger picture—the why—eluded her.

“Commander,” Sienna said quietly, “the people are scared. They need direction. They need a lie, if the truth isn’t ready yet.”

For a heartbeat, the temptation flickered—how easy it would be to calm them with a half-truth. But the cost of that lie felt heavier than any fear. She would not trade truth for temporary comfort—no matter her own fear.

“They will have the truth,” Anara insisted, pushing away the cynicism.

But a sliver of fear worked its way into her heart, a tiny, cold wire of doubt. What else is coming? She had never felt so utterly blind.

Below, riots spiked again as night fell. Black-market water traded hands at extortionist rates. Fistfights broke out over dwindling supplies. Paranoia was the true infection.

Police drones scanned the crowds, their searchlights harsh and unforgiving.

A voice shouted above the noise: “Rhodor wants us divided—you’re handing them victory!”

But the answer came sharp and immediate: “How do we know someone here didn’t help them? We can’t trust anyone!”

Paranoia spread like poison, dissolving the bonds of Artorian society faster than any virus.

As the hours dragged on toward dawn, the command center dimmed further under emergency lighting. Officers slumped in chairs. The few remaining active screens flickered weakly, spitting out streams of corrupted, meaningless data. Anara felt the crushing weight of professional defeat. They had stabilized the physical world—barely—but a ghost still owned the systems.

Anara stepped onto the observation walkway, staring out at Novar's vast, dark surface. The city was a sea of scattered, frightened lights. We're holding—for now. But if Rhodor pushes harder…

She turned back to the consoles with renewed resolve, determined to find one clean thread.

Returning to her station, she scrolled through the few non-corrupted packets of code Joric had saved. Line after line of digital wreckage, useless as ash.

Then, a pattern emerged from the peripheral data—not in the core financial code, but in a secondary log file for fusion reactor diagnostics.

Too precise.

Too patient.

Too familiar.

A cipher blinked in the corner of the log—one she recognized from Veyra's earliest, experimental work on long-range targeting systems. But this wasn't Veyra's. It was a mirror image, a malicious echo. And it was integrated with a geo-locator pinging the Artorian Fusion Core.

Her breath caught, fear turning into a cold, diamond-hard certainty. She leaned closer, whispering to herself:

"This wasn't an attack on our economy…"

Her pulse quickened, the truth burning away all her fatigue.

"…it was an opening act."

She looked up at the main map, seeing the scattered lights of Novar—all the panic, all the death, all the riots—as a necessary distraction for the enemy to place one, singular, fatal piece of code. Anara gave a final, low-voiced line to the empty, wounded room.

"Rhodor wasn't trying to cripple us today… They were softening the ground."

Chapter 12

BURNING SKY

Sirens had dissolved into a continuous, high-pitched shriek of total system overload. From the Command Center's reinforced balcony, Commander Anara Artoria stared out at the city she was losing. Her knuckles were white, gripping the cold steel railing against the background of a sickening, strobing red light that pulsed across Novar's burning horizon. The assault wasn't just noise; it was a physical force, a deep, persistent tremor that ran up through the soles of her boots, threatening to shake her composure apart.

The air in the Command Center was heavy, thick with the metallic tang of hot, overloaded circuitry. Below, Novar writhed in its death throes. Plumes of black, oily smoke rose like monstrous, broken pillars, suffocating the emergency beacons that now blinked in a slow, panicked, futile rhythm.

Below the balcony, the evacuation convoys were chaos given form. Families pressed against locked transport bays, their voices rising in a single, wordless plea that pierced even the shriek of bombardment. A medic stumbled past a burning shuttle, his gloved hands still slick with someone else's blood.

They're not numbers, Anara reminded herself, even as the tactical feed rendered them as such—fading blue icons, disappearing by the dozen. They are the pulse we're losing with every order I give.

Inside the war room, the atmosphere was pressurized, desperate chaos teetering on the edge of panic. Tactical officers moved like shadows across the holo-maps, their faces illuminated by the frantic, shifting blue and red light of the projections. Every display screamed a litany of failure: POWER FLUCTUATIONS. CRITICAL BREACH. STRUCTURAL INTEGRITY IS LOW.

"Commander Artoria—Sector Seven reports heavy casualties," a voice, raw with strain, screamed over the primary comm channel. The static was so dense it felt like grit in the ear. "We're losing the barricades! Estimated hold time: four minutes at best!"

"Understood. Divert remaining automated fire to cover Sector Seven's withdrawal," Anara replied. Her tone was a sheath of cold control—each word deliberate, an anchor against the rising tide of fear. I am calm. I am the steel.

She found Senator Aurek Tyrell at the command dais, perfectly dressed, his suit now a ridiculous contrast to the chaos. He didn't wear the look of a commander, but of a financier watching a bad investment collapse.

"Artoria," Tyrell said, his voice cutting through the noise, "your strategies are proving fatally reactive. This city is a liability. We need to secure the resources that guarantee our long-term survival."

Anara strode to the dais, ignoring the tremors beneath her feet. "The Rhodorians are adapting. But if we pool the last of the power to defend the central fusion grid—"

Tyrell scoffed, waving a dismissive hand at the frantic holo-map. "An alliance? With you? You cling to sentiment, Commander. I control the budget and the critical fleet reserves. Tell me, what is the strategic value of preserving a mob when the government meant to lead them is lost?"

"The value is the lives you swore to protect," Anara countered, her voice dangerously low. "If we use the power you are hoarding, we can hold the grid long enough to secure full civilian evacuation. I need immediate authorization to reroute secondary energy reserves to the transport fleet's auxiliary thrusters."

Tyrell finally looked away from the console and met her gaze, his eyes coldly reflective. "I have already calculated the maximum viable rescue, Anara. The math has reached its final, cruel verdict, and it does not favor the masses. There are only enough working shuttles and enough fuel to save the Artorian future—the Council, the scientists, the essential personnel. The populace is, regrettably, statistical noise."

"The Artorian future is the populace!" Anara erupted, her composure finally fracturing. "You will authorize the power transfer now. That is an order under wartime emergency protocol."

Tyrell smiled—a thin, chilling expression of absolute political power. "And my command authority supersedes yours regarding resource allocation. I am interested in preserving the assets that will allow us to win the next war. You are obsessed with saving the people who will die in this one."

Through the command feed, Anara pulled up multiple live visuals: helmet-cam streams from soldiers, traffic drone footage, even hacked civilian broadcasts. The lower levels of Novar were a maelstrom.

Artorian troopers fought house to house, the air thick with plasma haze. Civilians surged toward broken transport gates, their faces streaked with ash. The city's emergency loudspeakers still repeated the evacuation mantra—"Remain calm, the grid is stabilizing"—even as the grid itself began to burn.

A camera feed flickered to an empty school courtyard where a group of children huddled around a dead security drone, its once-glowing eyes dark. For a moment, Anara couldn't look away. This is what Tyrell calls noise, she thought. This is the sum of his arithmetic.

She killed the feed and turned back to the maps, jaw set. Compassion would have to wait until morning—if morning came.

Kael's last report came through in fragments—his voice breaking between bursts of weapons fire.

"We're holding," he said. "Barely. I've got twenty men still mobile. They're fighting like they were born in fire."

"Then make it count," Anara replied. "Every minute you hold is another life offworld."

"Copy that," he said, and then, softer, "Don't let them forget us, Commander."

Anara froze at the sound—Kael never said please, never sought remembrance. She wanted to respond, but static swallowed his words, leaving only the distant percussion of war echoing through dead channels.

Another violent shudder rippled through the Command Center. A massive crack split a nearby viewport, tracing a jagged line across the city's burning reflection. A display panel sputtered, showering sparks onto the floor before plunging into darkness. The air vents seized up completely, leaving the air immediately stifling and heavy.

Anara connected to the deep-level comms for the Fusion Grid engineers, and the sound that filled her ear was pure, unadulterated terror.

"—Primary shielding is cycling down! I can't stabilize the shunt! Regulators are melting—I'm getting a complete thermal failure on Seven!"

"Forget the shielding! Divert everything—everything—to the main Grid support beams! Buy Kael's team ten more minutes to clear the perimeter! We can't let this thing implode early!"

The sound of the Grid collapsing was a living thing—low and hungry. The floor vibrated with it, a subsonic growl that worked its way into the bones. Somewhere deep beneath Novar, the reactors screamed, a mechanical wail that rose through the ducts like the cry of a dying god.

Screens showed power routing erratically—currents jumping circuits, burning out entire sectors in chain reactions that looked almost organic. Sparks rained from the ceiling like false stars.

Anara could hear the screaming proximity alarms, the roar of venting steam, and the hopeless voice of the chief engineer: "It's too late. The structural integrity is failing from the inside!"

She looked at Tyrell, whose attention was now wholly consumed by his personalized datapad. He was confirming the lockout, ensuring Anara could not access the reserve power he planned to use for his own flight.

"General Kael's forces are taking critical casualties, Commander!" an officer yelled, tears streaming down his face as he watched the red icons vanish from the tactical map. "They are cut off and surrounded! They are requesting a final, immediate extraction!"

Anara closed her eyes, forcing Kael's calm face from her mind. "Denied." She knew there would be no return from this choice. "They hold the line until the transports breach the atmosphere." She opened her eyes, fixing them on Tyrell. "Unlock the civilian power now, Senator, or I will arrest you for treason."

Tyrell finally clicked his datapad shut. “I am not interested in your theatrics, Commander.” He retrieved a sleek, armored briefcase—the physical backup of his political life. “The Council transports are prepped and awaiting my departure signal. I have secured the future, Artoria. The only treason is your stubborn adherence to a lost cause.”

Before Anara could move, two large security guards, Tyrell’s personal detail, materialized silently behind him. He gave a curt nod and strode toward the high-security escape corridor.

“I regret your choice, Artoria. Enjoy the silence,” Tyrell said, his words vanishing as the blast doors hissed shut behind him. He had abandoned Novar, not in panic, but in calculated, political triumph.

Deep in the undercity, the Fusion Core’s containment field faltered and reignited in erratic pulses. Engineers scrambled through corridors that glowed like the veins of a dying star.

“Pressure surge on line three!” someone screamed.

“Vent it through the coolant towers—now!” another shouted back.

Anara could almost feel their panic echoing through the comm frequencies. The sound of failure wasn’t just alarms—it was human breath, quick and uneven. She wanted to be down there with them, hands on the controls, fighting beside them. Instead, she stood in a silent room of screens, watching their heartbeats blink out one by one.

"I'm sorry," she whispered to the static. "You built the world we lost."

Anara was left alone with the dying. The floor beneath her feet began to tear—a grinding sound of structural plates shearing apart. The main holographic projector convulsed violently, turning the battle display into a meaningless, blinding blur before it died with a final, painful crack.

A separate, non-Artorian frequency blinked on her personal console. A malicious, final transmission from the victor. Kess.

She connected the feed, bracing herself. The screen resolved to a desolate, fire-lit street corner. General Kael knelt there, bloodied and broken, but his eyes still locked forward in absolute defiance. Rhodorian Seekers rang him.

General Kess stood over him, his obsidian armor gleaming, an inhuman shadow cast by the flames. Kess looked directly into the camera, his gaze never wavering—tactical, and utterly devoid of pity.

"Let the ashes of their defiance remind the Artorian regime what happens when order is defied," Kess's voice hissed, intended for Anara alone—a private declaration of victory. "Fire."

The plasma blast hit Kael's chest. The light of the weapon was the last bright thing Anara would see in Novar. The screen went dark, dissolving into static and then nothing.

She waited for the grief, for the rage, for something human to rise—but there was only the quiet click of cooling metal. Her pulse sounded distant, alien, as if it belonged to someone else.

So this is what survival feels like, she thought. Hollow. Weightless. Louder than death.

The final catastrophe followed instantly. The Fusion Grid—already destabilized by the fighting and starved of power by Tyrell's lockout—went critical. It convulsed, not with an explosion, but with a terrifying, protracted implosion. A final, blinding emerald flash erupted from the city's depths, followed by a seismic, gut-wrenching groan that sounded like a mountain falling.

Every light, every fan, every system in the Command Center died at once. The deep, continuous hum of power—the lifeblood of the city—vanished.

Novar was plunged into absolute, total darkness and the resulting, horrifying silence.

Anara Artoria, surrounded by the crushing heat, was the last flicker of resistance in the room.

"Emergency comms," she ordered, her voice a low, rough rasp, yet carrying the terrible, cold weight of command. "Patch me through to all remaining units. Secure the channel. No Rhodorian interference."

She gripped the portable communicator, its tiny red display the last beacon. "Artorian forces, this is Commander Artoria," she said, tone steady, defiant. "We are not defeated. Novar is lost. Implement Blackout Protocol, all sectors. Evacuate and regroup on perimeter moons. Civilians have priority. We fight another day."

The occupation was quiet, methodical, and final. Hours passed—or perhaps a lifetime.

When Anara finally stepped out into the ruined, ash-covered streets, the fires had stopped consuming and were now merely burning, turning the vast, starless sky a perpetual, sickly orange. Rhodor's dagger-shaped drones drifted overhead, mechanical carrion birds, their shadows slicing across the rubble.

The wind carried the faint sound of distant engines—occupation drones sweeping the ruins for survivors. Each pass made her shoulders tense, but she didn't flinch. There was no one left to flinch for.

Somewhere beneath the rubble, the Fusion Grid's molten core still pulsed, a weak green light flickering through the cracks. A heart that refuses to stop, she thought. That's what we become now.

Tyrell, somehow, managed to find her in the makeshift command post of the ruined market district. His suit was now genuinely damaged, ash-streaked, but his face was grimly composed. He returned not to help, but to claim the narrative.

"Rhodor has shown us what division costs," he murmured, keeping his voice soft for the handful of exhausted, ragged survivors nearby who watched them with dead eyes. "Our infighting made this inevitable. You see the result of sentimental choices."

Anara's voice was soft, dangerously so, carrying the echo of Kael's final breath. "A lesson paid in blood. My blood—and Kael's."

Tyrell dismissed the loss with a faint wave of his hand. "And blood buys opportunity. The people will need new leadership after this. Leadership that understands the cold necessity of command and the value of preserved assets. I am the sole surviving official of the Council."

Anara turned toward him slowly. Her eyes, reflecting the dying firelight, held only a terrifying, absolute clarity. "The dead decide who leads now, Senator," she said, her voice a low, unshakable promise. "Not the survivors who ran."

He stiffened, the politician's smile vanishing entirely. "I have secured the government-in-exile, Commander. I have secured the future of Artoria."

Anara climbed a mound of shattered, fire-scarred plasteel and looked down on the ruined capital—her home. Novar was gone, but something colder, sharper had taken root in her chest. The city had fallen because of the weakness of men like Tyrell and the calculated ruthlessness of men like Kess.

You broke us, Kess.

You stripped away everything I valued.

But you taught me how to win.

She walked the ruins in silence long after Tyrell retreated to whatever bunker he would call a throne. Every step crunched over glass and bone. The once-mirrored towers of Novar were now jagged silhouettes against the red dawn—monuments to arrogance.

A single Artorian banner, half-burned, clung to the spire of a fallen shuttle. It flapped weakly in the sulfur wind.

Anara stopped beneath it, watching the fabric tear itself apart thread by thread.

We built a world that believed it was unbreakable, she thought. *Now we know what we're made of.*

She turned from the banner and stared east, toward the black horizon where Rhodor's fleet hovered like a wound in the sky. "You think you've won," she murmured. "But you've just given me the reason I needed."

Then, turning back to Tyrell and the small band of survivors below, she spoke, her voice carrying the cold authority of a newly forged leader. "We rebuild," she said simply. "And when we do—we don't forgive. We don't forget the cost that survival demanded."

Anara stood unflinching against the glow. This wasn't a defeat. It was a transformation. The soft, moral heart of Artoria had been incinerated in the fires of Novar. In its place beat an iron heart.

Chapter 13

SIEGE OF TENEBRIS

Anara Artoria's figure stood as a bulwark of determination against the doubt that threatened to engulf her team, her silhouette cutting through the shifting shadows of the temporary command post. As she spoke to her strike team, the faint light from the portable holoscreens cast sharp angles across her face.

"Tonight, we reclaim the capital city of Tenebris," Anara said, her voice steady and commanding in the small room. "They're using Rhodor's command center as a chokehold. Cut off the head, and the body will starve."

She glanced over her team—battle-worn armor, faces set like carved stone. Each of them carried the same quiet resolve reflected in her eyes. "We move in silence. Precision is our weapon. Our primary target is the central command node. But our deeper mission…" She tapped the holo-map where a pulsing red dot marked the sub-level archives. "The truth is buried down here. We take it."

Weapons were checked one last time. Armor sealed. Breath steadied. They moved out through the cracked and broken streets of Tenebris—once a thriving metropolis, now a shattered field of ruins where even the wind seemed to move carefully, afraid to disturb the dead.

Shattered spires loomed overhead like broken teeth. Entire plazas had sunk where bombardments gutted the city's foundation. In that ruin, Anara and her team slipped through the shadows like phantoms.

Tonight, the silence belonged to them.

General Kael advanced across the outskirts of the capital like an omen carried on steel boots. Behind him, Artorian soldiers marched in silent synchronization, their armor etched with soot and old blood. The blackout sky above them flickered with distant fire.

"Sync watches," Kael ordered. The wind barely carried the words; it was enough.

On his wrist, a glowing tactical map cast the ridges of his scarred face in unforgiving light. "Demolition teams—you have your marks. We ignite everything at 0300. Make it bright enough to blind their gods."

The attack was not for victory. It was for chaos.

The first shriek of inbound plasma tore through the night. Kael did not flinch.

"Positions!" he roared.

The battlefield exploded into color—crimson bolts slicing the darkness, cerulean streaks burning the air.

Rhodorian sentries were vaporized where they stood, their armor folding like foil.

A shell slammed into the ground, sending two soldiers sprawling. Kael was already there, grabbing one by the collar and dragging him behind a broken barrier.

“Ridge line!” Kael barked. His rifle snapped to his shoulder. Three controlled bursts—three visors shattered.

They advanced through a storm of debris.

A thermite charge detonated at the fuel depot door, spewing molten metal. Kael led the breach, the entryway awash in boiling sparks. Inside, the fighting collapsed into close quarters—rifle butts, blades, fists, and panic-tight grunts.

A Rhodorian lunged at him with a vibro-blade. Kael sidestepped, seized the man’s wrist, and drove the blade into the seam beneath the soldier’s helmet.

Another enemy tackled him to the ground. They rolled through grime and shrapnel. A punch cracked against Kael’s jaw. He answered with a brutal headbutt, followed by a rebar shard jammed into the gap beneath the soldier’s arm. The man spasmed once, then fell limp.

Kael rose into the blazing orange glow of a ruptured fuel line. Behind him, the entire depot roared like a dying beast.

Above, drones screeched. Two Reaper units descended, pulse cannons blazing.

“Sky-Breaker—now!”

One of Kael’s drones launched a missile that split the night, ripping through the first Reaper. It collapsed into flaming wreckage, its falling mass crushing the second unit below. The resulting explosion bathed the desert in a sunburst.

The shockwave blasted Kael off his feet. His HUD glitched, sound collapsing into a ringing void. Through the haze, he saw a young soldier dragging a comrade to cover while laser bolts traced death-patterns across the dirt.

That same soldier hesitated as a wounded Rhodorian reached for a sidearm.

Kael strode over, took the boy’s rifle, and fired two bolts into the Rhodorian’s skull.

“No hesitation,” Kael said, returning the rifle. “They wouldn’t spare you.”

Around him, civilians peered from the ruins, hollow-eyed specters of war. Kael didn’t look at them. Mercy was a luxury men like him were not allowed.

Tonight, he was the monster they required.

The fight ended in smoldering ruin. Fires crackled among melted girders. The wind moaned through what had once been homes.

A young lieutenant approached, face streaked with ash.

“Sir… the civilian sector took drone collateral damage. There are people in there.”

Kael didn’t slow. “There are no civilians in a warzone, Lieutenant. Only combatants and casualties.”

He nodded toward the Rhodorian dead being stacked in rows.

“This is the language they understand.”

His words hung colder than the night air.

Kael walked on.

Blocks away, Anara crouched at the entrance to Rhodor’s command hub. Her strike team waited in perfect stillness behind her.

Two guards patrolled the entry.

A silenced dart whispered through the night, dropping the first. The second turned—too slow. A shadow rose behind him, snapping his neck with a clean twist.

Anara moved swiftly, retrieved the keycard from the guard’s belt, and signaled.

The door unlocked with a soft click. Timing was everything. They slipped inside.

The hum of machinery vibrated through the metal floor—the heartbeat of Rhodor's occupation. Amber lights cast long shadows across the corridors.

Anara raised her fist. The squad froze.

They were inside the beast.

While Anara advanced deeper into the command center, the space battle above Tenebris reached its crescendo.

On the Rhodorian flagship The Dominator, Admiral Kess watched tactical readouts with a predator's grin.

"Target their lead cruiser. Break their spine."

But the Artorians had teeth of their own.

A blast from a stealth frigate ripped through the Dominator's flank. Sirens wailed across the bridge as emergency lights bathed everything in red.

"Spectral signatures everywhere!" a sensor officer shouted. "They're coming out of concealment!"

Kess snarled. The Spectral Net had turned the Artorian fleet into ghosts.

But the victory was not bloodless.

"The Valiant Heart is gone," someone cried over Anara's comms. A fiery bloom lit the orbital darkness as the ship tore apart. Anara's chest tightened—another cost added to the tally.

Kess pivoted the crippled Dominator. "Fire the forward lances! Target the Aegis Spire!"

A beam seared past Anara's flagship, grazing the shields.

She didn't flinch.

"Strike their engines. Torpedoes—now!"

The Aegis Spire spat a salvo of photon torpedoes, hammering the Dominator's weakened flank.

Kess was thrown to the deck as his ship buckled. Blood smeared across the console as he rose, eyes blazing.

"Retreat! Regroup!"

He fled, but Rhodor would remember this wound.

Anara opened all channels.

"This is Commander Anara Artoria. Tenebris is not yours to take. You tried to break us. You failed."

Her message echoed across every Rhodorian frequency.

And then she cut the line.

Alarms erupted overhead.

Kess had triggered a remote self-destruct.

"Move!" Anara shouted. Her team sprinted deeper into the command center as the floor shuddered beneath them. Explosions rippled through the structure. Sparks showered them. Metal groaned like an animal in pain.

They reached the archive vault and slammed the door behind them just as the command room above disintegrated.

Inside, flickering consoles and ancient data cores filled the small chamber. Deeper still, behind a sealed partition, they found something else—something older.

A slab of stone.

A glyph.

Not Rhodorian.

The lines shimmered beneath her fingers, rearranging like liquid.

Then a voice—quiet, cold, inside her bones.

Rumors spoke of artifacts older than Rhodor.

"You are not ready."

The glyph pulsed, showing—impossibly—her ancestor's face twisted in a silent scream.

Dr. Alyssa Artoria.

Then gone.

Her breath caught, and for a heartbeat, the war faded behind that face.

The glyph faded to darkness.

The silence afterward was heavier than the explosions.

When they emerged from the collapsing sub-levels into the half-destroyed lower plaza, Anara's team was met by a group of Tenebresian locals—those who had sold information to Rhodor during the occupation, identifying Artorian resistance members for execution.

Kael's men had rounded them up during the diversion.

Kael wasn't there. Only his shadow remained.

Six collaborators knelt in a row, hands bound, faces bruised. Anara recognized two men who had once distributed food in the relief district. Now they shook with fear.

An Artorian 9th officer shoved another collaborator forward. "Caught them signaling the Rhodorian patrols," he growled. "Orders?"

Anara's jaw tightened. She hated this part—the part Kael reveled in. But leaving them free meant more dead Tenebresians tomorrow.

"Stand them up," she ordered.

The soldiers yanked the prisoners to their feet. One tried to spit at her. An Artorian trooper drove a knee into his ribs, folding him with a strangled cry.

"Please—Commander—mercy—"

"You traded lives for rations," Anara said. "You traded children for safety. You knew what Rhodor would do with those names."

One man broke into sobs. Another stared defiantly.

"Do it," he spat. "Rhodor was right. You're weak."

Anara nodded once.

The soldiers moved.

It wasn't execution—Kael would've done that without blinking. It was punishment, deterrence, and very physical justice.

Gauntleted fists met bone. Prisoners hit the ground hard. The blows weren't designed to kill—just to break. Strikes landed with brutal efficiency.

When it ended, every collaborator lay face-down in the dirt, moaning or unconscious. Alive. Marked. Publicly broken.

"Release them," Anara said. "Let the city judge them now."

Her soldiers hesitated—they wanted blood—but obeyed.

The collaborators dragged themselves away, broken, watched by silent, grim-faced civilians.

Anara didn't enjoy it.

But tonight had no space for gentleness.

Back at the makeshift command post, news spread quickly.

"Tenebris is ours again," an officer said. "Kael eliminated all Rhodorian resistance."

"Spectral Net?" Councilor Elara asked sharply.

"A success," the tech officer replied.

"Then we push to Cygnus next," she said eagerly.

Councilor Naren's voice cut through her enthusiasm. "And when they build their own? What horrors will that unleash?"

Anara said nothing. Her mind returned to the glyph. To the voice.

To her mother.

Later, alone in the shattered tower overlooking the city's broken skyline, Anara whispered,

"Sleep while you can. Tomorrow… we rise."

The war wasn't over.

The war was changing.

And so was she.

Chapter 14

THE FRACTURED CROWN

The transport Aurelion cut a pale wound through Tenebris' copper sky, contrails smearing into the electrical haze. In the aftermath of Tenebris' fall, the planet's sky had become a silent witness to the war's new chapter, the lightning now revealing what was once hidden. Its form was blurred at the edges, masked by the faint shimmer of the Spectral Net—the same technology that had won the void, now hiding their presence on the ground.

Inside, the cabin lights were dialed down to a surgical dim. Armor buckles clicked. Filters hissed. The scent of charged dust rode the recycled air.

"Approach vector locked," Lieutenant Sera said, thumbs hovering above thruster paddles.

"Minimal turbulence," Captain Veyra Shiran added, eyes on a column of jittering numbers. "By Tenebrisian standards, that's 'only probably fatal.'"

A few strained smiles. Not humor—pressure relief.

Anara Artoria stood at the viewport, her reflection a ghost floating over the planet's scarred basin. "Keep the scanners live," she said. "If the signature twitches, I want to feel it in my teeth."

Below them: a perfect circle where no geology dared be perfect. Glassed ridges folded away from it like ripples frozen mid-breath. At the center: darkness that wasn't absence so much as intent. There was something else on this planet—something ancient that predated the Rhodorian conflict. The memory of the glyph from the command-center archive surfaced in her mind, cold and enigmatic. She could feel a similar presence here, a deeper whisper waiting beneath the planet's skin.

The Aurelion settled on its skids with a knuckled thud. The ramp is unsealed. Wind came in carrying dust that glittered like ground solder. When Anara's boots touched soil, she felt it immediately—a subsonic murmur, the low throb of a sleeping machine. Beneath her calm stirred a ripple of curiosity, the unsettling sense that they had awakened something far older than the conflict at hand.

"Geothermal?" General Kael asked, visor haloing his voice.

Veyra shook her head. "No. Pulse is too regular. Sixty-one seconds, stable amplitude, rising… there." The scope ticked. "Rising again."

Dr. Leira Thane knelt by a jagged fissure. She brushed its edge clean with a gloved hand. “This isn’t rock.”

Anara came down beside her. “Say that again.”

“It’s lattice,” Leira said. “Synthetic carbon in a recursive, fractal stacking. Grown, not cast. The binding impurities are… deliberate.” She paused, reluctant to finish the thought. “It’s closer to tissue than concrete.”

“Biological architecture,” Anara said.

Leira nodded. “If I’m right, Commander—this isn’t a ruin. It’s alive.”

The next pulse hit—not with sound, but with pressure, a slow tide climbing through bone. Seams in the ground lit from within: thin gold threads running out in long rays from the crater, joining and rejoining until the entire plain became a luminous web.

“Recording,” Veyra said, breathless despite herself. “Telemetry synced. Amplitude spike… spike… and—”

The light brushed their suit bands, and every biomonitor on the team flashed green. For an instant, the pulse synchronized with the rhythm of their hearts.

“It’s mapping us,” Kael murmured.

Anara’s hand hovered over her sidearm, reflex useless against geology that wasn’t. “We have what we came for. Pack samples, seal cores, and go back to the ramp. I don't want to be here when it asks a better question."

They moved fast and clean. The Aurelion swallowed them whole. As the ramp rose, the hum deepened from curiosity to… focus. On Veyra's console, the pattern coiled into a spiral and held—no longer a heartbeat, something more patient.

No one saw the matching spiral etched in dust beneath the landing strut. The wind licked it away.

"Tower, this is *Aurelion*," Sera said. "We're wheels up."

Anara kept her eyes on the basin until the crater slid under the wing and the gold veins blurred to a warm bruise in the planet's skin.

"Whatever that is," she said quietly, "it isn't asleep anymore."

As they ascended, a report from Kael's ground forces scrolled across a secondary screen—a terse summary of "pacification" with overwhelmingly one-sided casualty figures. Anara's victory in orbit had been precise, a surgical removal of a threat. Kael's was a butcher's bill, written in blood and ash. She had cut off the head of the enemy in space; he had chosen to salt the earth on the ground. The duality of their war—the strategist and the scourge—left a cold weight in her stomach.

The war room's great lens showed a holosweep of Colonial Nine: blue beads for protected worlds, amber for contested, and two ash-gray where the lights had gone out. Engineers murmured around the Aegis Array's status ring—its deep, almost musical hum threading the room like a memory of safety.

"Commander," the comms officer said. "Rhodorian flagship Devastator requests live exchange. Priority mark scarlet."

Anara took her place at the dais. "Put him on."

General Daeron Kess rose in the projection like a statue from a flooded courtyard—edges wavering, face carved in restraint rather than triumph.

"Artoria," he said. "You've delayed the inevitable long enough. Surrender your fleets, your weapons, and your leader. Do that, and your oceans will go unboiled."

"You already tried to boil them," Anara said, not blinking. "They're still wet."

A muscle in Kess's jaw ticked—irritation, or respect for the audacity. Hard to tell with men who learned their expressions from knives.

Behind him, a junior officer leaned in. "Commander, long-range—"

Kess lifted one finger without looking. The officer subsided.

"You fight well," Kess said to Anara. "You also know the arithmetic. End it before I do."

The line crackled, the projection lagging by a heartbeat as Novar's defensive jammers breathed.

"We'll end it," Anara said. "But not on your schedule."

Kess's eyes narrowed. Another officer tried again—urgent now, pointing at a corner of the tactical board just off-frame.

"Speak," Kess snapped, not turning this time.

"Flickers in the magnetosphere, sir," the officer said. "Atmo-glint along high vector lanes. It looks like—"

The lights on Devastator's bridge fluttered. Kess didn't notice the way the starfield behind him seemed to thicken, like frost forming on glass.

"It looks like ships," the officer said, voice very small.

They hit at once. Not a volley—a curtain.

Artorian frigates fell out of the magnetosphere like thrown knives, heat shrouds tearing away in sheets of white flame. Raptor-class cruisers rolled into the holes the frigates made and spat ion lances at point-blank range. The first Rhodorian carrier broke open like a geode, its hangar bleeding fire and men.

"Signal bloom!" Veyra shouted over the room's rising roar. "Spectral Net is live!"

On Kess's screens, phantom signatures multiplied, turrets firing into space as real hulls slipped through blind corners.

"Adjust frequency," Kess barked.

"They're hopping with us!" his gunnery chief cried. "Sir, they're tracing our sweep and skipping harmonics a half-beat ahead!"

Above Novar, the Valiant led a wedge through the enemy's middle guard, its flanks draped in flickering decoys. Captain Toren leaned into his harness, voice raw.

"Group Orpheus, mark targets, fire by feel—don't wait for locks! Skyfire, flood their coils—three-second burns, then cold!"

The space between fleets turned to shrapnel and hard light. Plasma torpedoes went in low, knifing under shield lips. Kess's rightward screen became a daisy chain of failures: coolant exsanguinating, coils spiking, comms nodes blinking to dead.

Boarding pods launched from the Valiant's belly, mag-grapples biting into the crippled cruiser as Artorians poured through the smoke-filled corridor. Sergeant Halet toggled his external mic. "Open your door, you iron bastards," he said. "We brought a housewarming."

A Rhodorian lance bit into Valiant's prow. The ship rang like a bell. Toren's world flashed white, then red—alerts, then blood.

"Hold the line," he said through his teeth. "We are the line."

At Novar, Kael's hands moved with a practiced calm that had nothing to do with peace. "Shift Skyfire three degrees. Raptor Wing, fold and punch—now. Group Echo, turn their flank into a corridor; leave them nowhere to run but into our teeth."

"Shields at sixty-seven," someone reported. "Aegis harmonics stable."

"Keep it singing," Veyra said, sweat dark in the cracks of her gloves. "If it goes flat, we all go silent."

"Commander," the comms officer called, throat tight. "We have Kess again—he's demanding surrender."

Anara didn't take her eyes off the main board. "Tell him we're busy."

"Bring batteries to bear!" Kess roared. "Load suppression rounds and detune to—"

He felt the hit in his teeth. A Raptor slid through Devastator's upper arc and raked the dorsal coils with a single long burn—surgical, obscene. The deck pitched. The forward viewport was crazed with silver lines and then held, a spiderweb that had decided—for the moment—to be glass.

"Status," Kess hissed.

"Dorsal coils are gone," Gunnery said quietly. "We can fight. We cannot reach."

"Then move," Kess said.

"Trims unresponsive," Helm replied. "We're a door with no hinges, sir."

The junior officer who had tried to warn him earlier straightened, jaw set. "Commander, request permission to engage fallback routine."

Kess stared at him for one long, feral second. He had built a career on never falling back. The word tasted like rust.

"Granted," he said, voice like gravel.

Across the Rhodorian grid, ships began to pivot into a shallow crescent—an old, reliable shape meant to bleed an attacker dry over time. Anara saw the curl forming.

"Do not let them close," she said. "Cut the bowstring."

Group Orpheus peeled away and came screaming cross-current, four ships wide, torpedoes slaved to Veyra's live-recalibrating feed. The first salvo tore the crescent's center out. The second drove a spear through the wound. The crescent folded into two dying hooks and then into ash.

Kess gripped the rail until his knuckles went bone-pale. The Devastator shuddered again—secondary explosions, not fatal, just humiliating.

He looked at the blank place on his tactical board where his ships had been.

"Open me to the Artorian Council," he said.

"Channel open," comms replied, voice thin with static and fear.

Kess's image rose again in Novar's chamber—smoke behind him now, alarms bleeding politely in the background.

"Artoria," he said. "Stand down. You've won a moment. You cannot win the day."

Anara didn't answer him. She watched the board and moved pieces he couldn't see.

"Commander," a Rhodorian officer whispered from off-screen, too quiet to be professional. "We're losing the rim guard. They're inside our spin."

Kess lowered his voice, so only his bride could hear. "Then spin faster."

On the Aurelion, leaving Tenebris's gravity well, Veyra ran the basin signature again, now that the battle telemetry fed into the same slate. Her screen overlaid the two waveforms: the spiral from the crater and the ghost-net frequency ladder used to spoof Rhodor's tracking.

They fit. Not a perfect copy—a call and answer.

Veyra blinked. "Anara," she said quietly. "The pattern we used to blind them? Tenebris gave us half that ladder before we knew to ask."

Anara didn't like coincidences. She liked debts even less. "Say that differently."

"It watched us," Veyra said. "Then it sang back in our key."

"How much did we teach it?"

Veyra looked at the numbers for a long time. "Enough to worry," she said. "Not enough to regret. Yet."

Anara watched the basin recede on the external cameras until even the bruise in the ground was gone. "Get our people home."

The battle widened and narrowed at once. In one sector, a Rhodorian dreadnought died slowly, its spine broken, venting fire like a comet bleeding daylight. In another, an Artorian frigate spun end over end, her nameplate—Crown of Dawn—flashing by between slabs of torn armor. Survival beacons chattered in a language both fleets could read: we're alive, we're alive, we're alive.

On the far edge, Cryostara's storms lit themselves for no one, lightning snarling around dark hulks drifting with their lights out. Somewhere aboard one of them, a pilot named Lira Odane lay half-strapped into a dead cockpit, whispering a joke to herself so she wouldn't scream. "Minimal turbulence," she mimicked Veyra's dry tone, and laughed once, which helped.

Back on Novar, the Aegis Array held its pitch—Zara Malik's old math still singing after two centuries. Engineers palmed hot capacitors and slotted cold ones in by touch, hands burned and smiling because the song hadn't stopped.

Kael leaned over the table and cut the enemy grid again and again until there weren't enough lines left to call it a grid. He slid a bead representing Valiant into a fallback arc, then moved it again when Toren refused politely by surviving forward.

"Losses?" Anara asked.

"High," Kael said. "Not fatal."

"Higher for them," Veyra added, without satisfaction.

"Then we breathe," Anara said, and only then noticed she hadn't done that in a very long minute.

Kess stood very still.

The bridge had quieted, not because the alerts had ceased, but because everyone had lost the old taste for shouting. Smoke curled in lazy question marks from a ruined console. A drip ticked somewhere, insistent.

"Status," Kess said.

"We can disengage," Helm said carefully. "We cannot pursue."

Kess nodded once, as if ruling on a minor procedural matter. In his chest, something cold clicked into place.

"Signal all units," he said. "Break contact by sectors. No routing. Every captain chooses their own hole. The ones who can make fire while running will do so."

The comms officer hesitated, then sent the order.

Kess turned his head, finally, toward the young officer who had warned him first. "You were right," he said.

"Sir?" the man managed.

"Don't savor it," Kess said. "It will not happen again."

He looked once more at the tactical, at the empty spots, and then away—as if refusing to memorize the shape of this humiliation.

“Open a private channel,” he said. “Commander Artoria and I will speak when the guns stop lying.”

The room’s roar decayed to a hum. People spoke in normal voices, surprised to hear themselves sound human.

On the lens, the Rhodorian formation fractured and thinned, leaving the dead behind with a miser’s stinginess. Artorian recovery beacons blossomed: tiny white stars in a sea of wrong light.

“Hold survivors as first-priority vectors,” Anara said. “No pursuit beyond the Aegis envelope. We bleed out if we chase a victory that isn’t there.”

Kael gave her a look that was approval-shaped like disagreement. “Aye.”

“Skyfire, begin drift-sweep,” Veyra added. “We’re not leaving our people in the dark.”

Anara’s gaze drifted to the far corner of the lens—Tenebris, now quiet, a little more itself than it had been in the morning.

“Captain,” she said to Veyra. “Say the thing you’re not saying.”

Veyra squared to her. “The basin learned us,” she said. “Not words. Structure. If we keep standing near it and thinking loudly, it will hum back in better keys.”

“And if Rhodor stands near it?” Kael asked.

"Then it will sing to them, too," Veyra said. "If they can stand the pitch."

Anara let the silence sit where everyone could see it. "We classify this as bone," she said finally. "Need-to-know means 'Anara says your name.' We move Aurelion's logs to the deep cold. Anyone who whispers Tenebris in a corridor gets reassigned to cleaning the outside of satellites with a toothbrush."

"Yes, Commander," Veyra said. She didn't smile.

Anara touched the old plaque set in the dais—Alyssa Artoria's favorite line, etched so deep the letters had their own gravity: We build to understand; we defend to develop again.

"Prepare to address the system," Anara said. "We tell the truth and none of the secrets. Grief first. Then resolve."

She looked up at the black ceiling—Novar's stars hidden by steel and necessity.

"Survivors," she murmured, a word like a hinge.

On Tenebris, far below the glassed basin, gold lines brightened in a rhythm that matched the battle's last twenty minutes, then shifted into a new measure no one alive could count. Microscopic machines rearranged, then waited. The spiral changed shape—just a touch—an artist's correction on a sketch not yet shown.

Beyond mapped lanes, farther out than charts bothered to promise, a sensor of unknown design registered the same rhythm and sent a single packet, encoded in geometry more than language. It crossed the dark like a needle through cloth.

No one on Novar saw it. Kess didn't, either.

But when it reached what it was sewing toward, something moved.

Chapter 15

A WORLD UNDONE

The secure tower room, usually a sanctuary of controlled light and silent data streams, was stifled by an oppressive stillness. The Artorian Council, dressed in ceremonial blacks and silvers for the upcoming wedding, gathered around the central holoscreen. The nuptials were minutes away, but General Daeron Kess had insisted this transmission could not wait.

Static hissed, a prelude to horror. Then Kess appeared, his projection dominating the space.

"Good evening, Council," he said, his tone a venomous calm, calculated to violate every diplomatic protocol. "I thought you might enjoy a gift before the ceremony."

The screen shifted to a desolate prison cell. General Kael knelt—bloodied, bound, yet utterly defiant. His eyes, even through the flickering holo-link, burned with cold challenge.

Anara gasped, the raw sound tearing from her throat, a stark contrast to the room's rigid composure. The room seemed to contract around her. Councilor Meron surged forward, his voice a tremor of official outrage. “This is a violation of every treaty—”

“I don’t care for treaties,” Kess cut in, his voice cold as a vacuum. “This is justice.”

Rhodorian guards, cloaked in heavy black armor, raised their plasma rifles. Their movements were slow, deliberate.

“No!” Anara cried, pushing past Meron, her hands outstretched in a futile gesture against the light and glass—but it was too late.

Kael lifted his head. His face was a grim mask of dried blood and resolve. His eyes locked with the Council—then found Anara. He swallowed once. “Don’t stop fighting.”

The shot came.

Kael fell.

The screen snapped to black.

Anara stood frozen, the last image burned into her vision. Her breath hitched—not in a cry, but in a strangled sound of pure, crystalline rage. Kael had been the dark mirror to her strategy, the one who carried the brutality so she didn’t have to. Now he was gone, and the calculus of survival was hers alone.

For a fleeting instant, something else stirred beneath the rage—not pity, not mercy, but a sharp sense of rupture, as if a line long under tension had finally snapped.

The silence did not last.

A siren wailed—not a fire alert, but a deep, structural shriek. A young technician, pale and shaking, burst into the room.

"Our orbital fleet—sir—the Aegis Dawn has imploded. The Resolute is gone."

"What?" Councilor Dareth barked, disbelief stripping the color from his face.

"The Spectral Net has been turned against us," the technician said, words tumbling. "Rhodor hacked our own system. The cloaking frequencies aren't just blocked—they're inverted. The energy feedback is catastrophic. Our weapons are coupling with our own fields."

Explosions echoed from the upper atmosphere—not incoming fire, but the dull, heavy sound of collapse. Through the tower's armored glass, fire blossomed across the sky above Artoria. Their greatest victory, purchased with forbidden science, was becoming their immediate undoing.

Anara felt certainty settle—cold, absolute. Kess hadn't just executed Kael. He had severed the advantage Kael died to protect.

The debt was due.

As the Council gathered in the secure tower room, the air was thick with the weight of their decisions. They knew the upcoming wedding, draped in ceremonial blacks and silvers, wasn't merely a union of two houses. It was a desperate political bid, a lifeline thrown against mounting losses. Every gesture, every alliance, was aimed at survival—a way to shield their people from the encroaching storm. The ceremony was leverage, meant to keep Artoria self-governing and out of Rhodorian hands.

She turned from the window, pulling the silver ceremonial veil from her head and letting it fall to the floor like a forgotten shroud. Her voice was quiet, decisive, and final.

"I'm going down there. The ceremony is commencing. I have a wedding to attend."

The ceremonial hall was a deceptive portrait of peace. Polished marble reflected cold, illusory light, and the scent of imported incense struggled to mask the faint tang of fear and ozone. General Daeron Kess stood at the altar, cloaked in imperial Rhodorian robes, posture smug beneath his silver coronet.

Anara entered slowly, clad only in the stark white of her ceremonial gown. Her steps were deliberate—a march into treason. Beneath the folds of her skirt, her fingers closed around the cold, familiar hilt of a custom-forged vibro-dagger.

She kept her gaze forward, bypassing Kess long enough to mark every guard, every delegate, every structural support. Every Rhodorian face wore calculated victory; every Artorian face held terror strained into hope.

The Artorian Council was already seated, pale and hollowed by execution and disaster. They expected her to surrender. They needed her to save them.

Kess extended his hand, a gesture of ownership. She accepted it with a cold, firm grip.

The Rhodorian priest began the rites—a grotesque fusion of two cultures. Anara barely heard him, the silence of her own intent drowning out the words.

…for the unity of our worlds… for the binding of houses Artoria and Rhodor…

Her breath steadied. The pulse in her fingertips sharpened. Beyond the shielded walls, distant weapons throbbed like a buried heart. This was not panic. It was a focus.

The priest turned to her, voice amplified. "Do you, Princess Anara, accept this bond for peace everlasting?"

The silence stretched. In that single beat, she saw Kael's bleeding chest. She saw the Spectral Net collapse. She saw her mother's dream of Artoria swallowed by Thorn Valik's hatred.

Peace is a lie, Kael's voice whispered in memory.

Her fingers found the hilt beneath the silk. As the priest's final word hung, she moved.

And drew the dagger.

A collective gasp swept the hall. She lunged—aimed for Kess's heart—but a Rhodorian guard fired instantly. The suppression bolt struck her shoulder, burning through fabric and flesh.

She cried out. The dagger carved only a shallow line across Kess's side—a wound, not a killing blow.

Chaos erupted. Guards shouted. Blaster fire scarred marble. Guests screamed and scattered.

Anara dropped to one knee, gripping her wounded arm. She looked up—Kess was already retreating, bloodied but alive, encircled by elite guards.

An Artorian officer grabbed her. "Commander! We have to move!"

"No," she spat, pain sharpening her fury. "We're not done."

But the room was flooding with Rhodorian soldiers. Councilor Meron activated an emergency beacon, the high-pitched shriek signaling a counter-contingency. "Initiate Phase Zero! Evacuate the chamber!"

Anara was dragged to her feet as Artorian elite guards—trained for this moment—shielded her with plasma arcs. The assassination attempt was confirmed as a planned contingency, a final, desperate gamble to decapitate the enemy.

Kess, clutching his bleeding side, shouted across the smoke-choked hall, his voice raw with a fury that promised eternal war. "This is treachery! The alliance is broken! Artoria will burn!"

Anara shouted back, her voice ringing with absolute defiance. "Then let it burn clean!"

They vanished down the corridor as the ceremonial hall collapsed under heavy fire, consuming the last pretense of peace.

The hidden door hissed shut behind them, muting screams and blaster fire to a dull, terrifying roar. The service tunnel was cold, thick with dust. Anara stumbled, her shoulder screaming in protest, and braced against the rough-hewn stone. The pristine white of her gown was now a ruin of soot, sweat, and the dark stain of her own blood.

Commander Thane Rho was at her side instantly, his grip firm on her uninjured arm. “Keep moving, Commander. They’ll be sealing the upper levels.”

She nodded and pushed off the wall, breath ragged as the adrenaline drained away, leaving a hollow, sickening ache. She had gambled everything on one strike and failed. Kael was dead. The fleet was in ashes. And she had declared open war in the most personal way possible. The weight of it pressed down on her, heavy enough to bend her spine.

“The others?” she managed, voice hoarse.

“A rear guard is holding the junction,” Rho said grimly. “We lost contact with Meron’s detail.” The unspoken truth hung between them: he was likely dead.

Another explosion shuddered through the tunnel, grit raining down. Anara closed her eyes for a heartbeat, then pushed forward. Grief was a luxury for those with time; she had none. Still, each step drove a fresh ache into her chest—a silent marker for the friend she had lost and the burden now hers alone.

Anara and her remaining guards emerged from the tunnels beneath the city. Her ceremonial robe was torn, her shoulder seared and crudely wrapped. The capital burned. Kael was dead. The fleet was shattered. And she was now the most wanted woman in the Artorian sector.

Hours later, shock had hardened into grim certainty. She stood alone in her private chamber in the hidden sector of Founders Tower.

She reached into a velvet pouch beneath her waist sash. The glyph. The small, hexagonal shard etched with alien patterns shimmered faintly. It had pulsed when Kael was executed. It had pulsed when the Spectral Net began to collapse. It was not passive; it observed, learning from pain and failure.

Now, in the quiet, it pulsed once. Not a warning—a response. As Anara's grief deepened, the glow intensified, its symbols shifting as if mirroring her turmoil.

She activated the holoscanner. The glyph lifted, rotating slowly. Lines of alien code spiraled around it—unreadable—until one symbol reconfigured itself.

The geometry defied known stellar mechanics, aligning not with star charts but with deep-space gravitational anomalies. It wasn't random. It was directional.

"It's a map," she breathed. A way out.

A knock followed.

"Enter."

Commander Thane Rho stepped in, Silver Guard armor still scarred from the ceremony. He saluted. "You shouldn't be on your feet, Commander."

"I've survived worse."

He hesitated. "We couldn't hold the chamber. Some of our people didn't make it out."

"I know," she said, distant. "Kael's death was a message. So is this."

She turned the holoscanner toward him.

Rho studied the swirling geometry, brow furrowed. "What am I looking at?"

"A warning," Anara said softly. "And an invitation."

She met his eyes. "It's leading us somewhere."

Rho raised an eyebrow, the disbelief competing with the disaster he'd just witnessed. "You want to follow it—now? After everything that just happened? We need to rally the remnants, prepare for the orbital siege."

"Commander, with respect, this is madness," Rho pressed, his expression grave. "We are facing an imminent planetary siege. Our command structure is in shambles. Our people need their leader here to organize the defense, to be a symbol of resistance. Not chasing ghosts on a map from a rock."

"A rock that reacted to our defeat, Commander," Anara shot back, her eyes flashing. She gestured to the burning cityscape visible through the reinforced window. "What defense? What resistance? Kess has already out-thought us, out-fought us. He turned our greatest weapon into our coffin. If we fight this war on his terms, with the tools he understands, we will lose. We are already losing."

She stepped closer, her voice dropping, low and controlled. "This is me organizing the defense. This is me finding a weapon he cannot comprehend, on a battlefield he doesn't know exists. Kael's final order was, 'Don't stop fighting.' This is the fight now. Not for this city, or this world, but for any future at all."

Rho held her gaze for a long moment, the distant alarms a constant reminder of their reality. He was a soldier of Artoria, sworn to defend its soil. What she was asking felt like desertion. But he had seen her brilliance—and he had just witnessed the total failure of conventional tactics.

"If we do this, we do it off the books. No transmission logs. No fleet tail. Just us. Traitors seeking a miracle."

"Just us," she agreed.

He studied her, the quiet trust between them new and fragile. "Where does it lead?"

She stared into the swirling projection. Symbols shifted again—forming a sigil older than Artoria itself.

"Beyond the Drift Belt. Into the Unclaimed Veil." The Drift Belt was a treacherous region of unpredictable gravitational storms and rogue asteroids—a black expanse of lost ships and forgotten lore.

Rho exhaled slowly, accepting the impossible scale of the mission. “Then I guess we’ll need a fast ship.”

She smiled, grim and battle-worn. “I know just the one. Prepare the Aurelion for deep-cold running. Maximum velocity.”

In the hangar, the Aurelion stood apart from the larger warships being frantically prepared for battle. Its sleek, scarred hull was being loaded not with troops or heavy munitions, but with long-range sensor pods and stealth equipment. The crew moved with quiet urgency, their faces set. They were no longer soldiers of the Artorian fleet; they were the hand-picked crew of a renegade ship on a near-suicidal mission.

Anara paused at the base of the ramp, looking back one last time at Founders Tower. Somewhere within its beleaguered heart, the Council was likely already debating her arrest for treason. She had sacrificed her legitimacy, her honor, and the last chance for peace. All she had left was a conviction colder than space—and a map to nowhere.

Rho stepped beside her, following her gaze. “They’ll call us traitors,” he said quietly.

"Let them," Anara replied, her voice flat. "History only remembers who wins."

She turned her back on her capital and walked up the ramp without a second glance.

Together, they turned toward the hangar bay, leaving behind the burning world and the human war, ready to chase a desperate, cosmic promise.

Chapter 16

INTO THE VEIL

The crystalline chamber felt alive. Not alive like flesh and blood—alive the way a black hole is alive: patient, ancient, hungry.

Dust drifted in slow silver sheets as Anara crossed the threshold. Each footstep echoed too loudly, like the moon itself was counting time in a language older than suns. The air tasted of old lightning—metallic, ionized—the residue of experiments that should never have been attempted.

Far above, muffled by kilometers of jagged moonrock, the orbital battle raged on. The Rhodorian armada was tightening its noose around the last free Artorian worlds. But here, at the forbidden heart of Varos, the world felt still. Suspended. Waiting.

Commander Thane Rho stepped in behind her, quiet as a ghost. His armor—once ceremonial silver—was now shattered, burn-scarred, half-melted. The left pauldron was gone, the underlying musculature bruised black and purple from shockwaves. Blood had dried in a long line down his jaw where shrapnel had grazed him earlier in the siege.

He looked like a man held together by duty alone.

At the center of the chamber, the glyph flared—an impossible, cold blue that made the air crease, like paper catching flame.

The light condensed—

—and Dr. Alyssa Artoria stepped out.

Twenty centuries dead. Still more awake than anyone Anara had ever known.

"Anara."

The voice rang like a struck bell—clear, resonant, impossibly alive. The chamber trembled, as if the name itself carried command.

"If you're seeing this, then the gentler futures I dreamed for our bloodline have collapsed. And you, my star, have been left with the hardest path."

Alyssa's eyes—Anara's eyes, generations removed—shimmered with starfields lost to time.

"We called it Veilfire," Alyssa said, her voice scarred by old fear.

"Not because it burns, but because it forces reality to misbehave."

The projection flickered, and the glyph behind her pulsed like a heartbeat falling into rhythm with her words.

"In its first phase, Veilfire destabilizes high-energy plasma fields. It strips electrons from their orbits, detonates fusion pockets, and turns hull metal into superheated particulate. You'll see it as light—violent, impossible light—tearing through anything with mass."

The chamber lights dimmed, as if the moon itself remembered.

"But the second phase…"

She looked down, unable to hide the dread.

"The second phase collapses the spacetime lattice itself. Gravity vectors invert. Bulkheads bend because the atoms in them can no longer agree on where 'solid' is. Structures scream as their molecular bonds are pulled in conflicting directions. Nothing explodes—it implodes. Slowly. Violently.

She drew a breath that wasn't a breath at all, only the echo of one.

"We banned it, Anara. Even in my era. Even at the height of our empire. Not out of morality—out of fear. We built Veilfire once… and swore never to awaken it again."

Her gaze lifted, sorrowful and resolute.

"That is why we feared it. Veilfire doesn't simply destroy. It erases stability. First the fire—then the forgetting."

The projection lifted a hand, fingers brushing Anara's cheek as if the light had weight.

"I hoped no child of our line would ever have to stand here," Alyssa whispered. "But hope is the first casualty of war."

The hologram fractured into a thousand upward-falling shards, dissolving into the vaulted darkness.

Silence fell like a curtain.

Anara looked at Rho—the man who had dragged her out of burning cities. The man who had trained her to survive when mercy died with the last daylight of Artoria.

"You can still walk away," she whispered. "This part is mine."

Rho stepped close enough that their ruined breastplates touched.

"I've walked away from everything else," he said, voice raw. "Not you."

Her hands shook as she unclasped her mother's pendant from around her neck. She folded it into his gauntlet.

"If anyone survives… make them remember we fought. Make them remember it wasn't surrender."

Rho pulled her into an embrace so fierce it hurt.

"You were the only orders that ever made sense," he breathed.

She turned from him before she lost her nerve.

Toward the pod. The coffin. The execution chair. The destiny her blood had sealed centuries before she was born.

It gleamed like a guillotine: perfect, cold, inevitable.

She had nearly reached it when the moon groaned.

A tectonic scream ripped through the chamber. Crystalline conduits burst like glass hit by hammers. The floor pitched sideways, throwing her hard to one knee.

For one heartbeat—a razor-thin sliver of living—she almost ran.

Then the memory hit.

Kael's forgiveness as Kess executed him.

Her little brother's cooling hand.

Her mother's last transmission:

Live long enough to make them regret it.

Anara stood.

She climbed in. The hatch sealed like the universe closing its last safe door.

Darkness swallowed her. Red emergency light throbbed like a failing pulse.

Cold gel climbed around her chest, thick and suffocating.

Then the world woke up screaming.

A metallic BANG detonated beneath her—

deep, seismic, like a hammer the size of a mountain striking an anvil of bedrock.

A second impact followed.

Then a third.

Each one closer.

Each one louder.

Steam roared through unseen conduits, venting in violent bursts that fogged the pod's glass from the outside.

The temperature spiked, then dropped, then spiked again—pressure systems slamming open and shut like furious lungs.

Somewhere below, colossal plates of compressed spacetime slammed into alignment, shrieking with the sound of tortured metal.

The moon's crust didn't shift—it was dragged, forced into position like a massive locking ring.

The chamber vibrated so hard her teeth ached.

A cascading series of clangs rang upward, like a forge firing to life, each metallic note echoing through the tunnels:

CHNG.

CHNG.

CHNG.

CHNG.

Then the roaring began.

Not air.

Not wind.

A tidal surge of superheated vapor ripping through gravitational vents—hot enough to blur vision, cold enough the next second to frost the walls.

The weapon wasn't activating.

It was breathing.

Glyphs flared around her pod, racing like molten metal cooling too fast, forming patterns that felt intentional—and terrifying.

Anara's spine pressed into the pod as a massive internal piston—or whatever passed for one—slammed forward, sending another metallic BOOM up through the chamber.

Her courage wavered.

This wasn't a device.

This was a forge built to kill gods.

Then the voice arrived.

Not language.

Not mercy.

DO YOU CONSENT TO BECOMING THE KEY?

She laughed once and tasted blood. Make them feel the weight of a single soul, she thought.

“Do I have a choice?”

The system accepted her answer.

Lightning erupted through her spine. Her back arched so hard something tore. Pain detonated behind her eyes. Her screams ricocheted around the pod, shredding her throat.

A second bolt.

A third.

A fourth.

Her memories peeled like burning pages. Her sense of self flickered.

Then the universe opened.

And swallowed her whole.

She saw the Rhodorian fleet—hundreds of capital ships, engines burning blue against a dying system.

She saw the Artorian refugee flotilla—packed, terrified, whispering prayers.

She saw Meridies wounded, cities broken open.

She saw Artoria cratered from orbit, yet somehow still alive.

She felt the Veil beneath reality, stretching, thinning, waiting.

She knew the price.

She paid it anyway.

THE BROADCAST (Emotion Sequence A)

The activation pulse erupted from Varos in a perfect expanding sphere—through rock, ship hulls, neural implants, radio channels, and memories.

Every comm in the system snapped to life.

Static.

Then:

Her scream.

Not human.

Not a machine.

Something caught between agony and transcendence.

Across the system, people froze.

On evacuation barges, parents clutched their children as tears carved clean tracks down soot-covered faces.

On the command deck of the cruiser Vanguard of Dawn, hardened veterans dropped to their knees.

Medics in overcrowded bays turned toward the speakers with horror.

Rhodorian deserters went pale.

Smugglers and pirates bowed their heads.

No translation was required.

They heard a woman dying for them.

They heard a soul breaking open.

They heard her words:

"The dark is rising… pulling me under… event horizon… the light is breaking…"

Her synapses burned out. Her vision dissolved. Her memories flickered away like dying lanterns.

With the last fragment of who she had been:

"INTO THE VEIL!"

The scream cut off—

Not fading, snapped, like a wire pulled too tight.

The silence that followed hit harder than any explosion.

And then there was only distance.

THE JUDGMENT

Reality did not break.

It buckled.

Ash

WAVE ONE — THE FORGE'S EXHALE

For the first second, the armada saw something they could understand:

An expanding front of superheated plasma and destabilized electrons, bright enough to bleach colors from vision.

This was the byproduct—the "steam" of the cosmic forge.

When it hit:

- Armor ionized instantly
- Hull plating vaporized
- Carrier ships peeled open like molten fruit
- Entire decks blew outward in sheets of incandescent debris

Dreadnoughts split along their spines, vomiting crew and atmosphere into space.

Thousands of soldiers didn't even have time to scream; the vacuum stole the air from their lungs before terror reached their eyes.

But then—

The light died.

And the real Veilfire began.

The beam did not fade.

It shifted phase.

Physics faltered.

Ships began to groan—

a low, terrible bending sound, like steel being persuaded to forget it was ever solid.

Bulkheads warped inward as molecular bonds lost consensus.

The support struts snapped, not due to stress, but because the gravity fields were inverting around them.

Some vessels exploded outward—

Their atoms are rejecting coherence and returning to atmospheric plasma.

Others imploded—

folding into themselves as the local spacetime lattice tightened like a fist.

Crew tore at harnesses, at escape pods, at each other—

Their bodies twisting as the gravity inside their ships changed direction mid-scream.

On the Devastator Prime, the spinal superstructure sheared in three places.

The lower decks folded inward like collapsing paper—

But the command spire tore free, emergency thrusters igniting in panicked bursts.

The spire tumbled into the dark, burning, spinning, mangled—

but intact.

Deep in the buckled ribs of the Devastator's spire, the dust began to settle. There was no movement, save for the erratic, metallic tick of a cooling engine.

But then—

Buried under a mile of glass and bone, a single, rhythmic thud echoed against the hull.

A ghost in the wreckage, refusing to stay silent.

In just four seconds:

- Three hundred capital ships
- Forty thousand escorts and supporters ceased to be ships.

They became gravitational residue scars burned into spacetime like smears on a cosmic lens.

They weren't destroyed.

They were disallowed.

And still the Veilfire wave burned on.

The forge roared.

The moon howled.

The universe trembled as the beam continued tearing through the last Rhodorian engine signatures for nearly a full minute.

Varos shuddered. Not from attack from **overload**.

The internal spacetime plates she had forced into alignment began to slip. One by one.

The moon didn't explode.

It collapsed.

A low, infrasonic groan rolled through space—felt more than heard

As the core structure lost stability.

Crustal plates rose, buckled, then tore free.

Kilometer-long fissures spidered across the surface, venting geysers of incandescent gas.

Then the central lattice failed.

A sphere of white-blue fusion blossomed outward—Not a fireball, but the visible aftermath of compressed dimensions snapping back to equilibrium.

Chunks of moonrock, some only meters wide, others the size of small mountains, detached and drifted into space on slow, terrible arcs.

Nearby ships were caught in the expanding debris halo:

- Some Artorian cruisers were torn apart
- Several refugee barges were damaged
- A few vessels were knocked from position, engines sputtering

- The orbital ring over Meridies fractured along one section but did not fall

But most of the fleet—those positioned farther out survived the blast zone, shaken and scorched but intact.

On Artoria, auroras flared blood-red, then faded.

And across the system, sensors registered a single truth:

Varos was gone.

Veilfire had consumed its cradle.

Rho dragged himself out of the collapsed tunnel, coughing up dust and blood.

Every muscle screamed

The air tasted like metal and ozone.

He staggered upright—and froze.

The sky was wrong.

Too dark.

Too empty.

As if someone had reached up and erased a moon out of the night, leaving the stars behind it shaken and out of place.

A medic sprinted toward him, sliding to a stop.

"Commander! We thought you were—"

"Status," he rasped, voice shredded.

The medic swallowed hard.

"Sir… the Rhodorian fleet is gone. Not disabled—gone. Just… signatures cut off mid-transmission. And Varos is—"

He glanced up at the empty patch of sky. "—there's nothing left to scan."

Rho stared at the void, jaw trembling despite him.

Slowly, he opened his hand.

Her pendant lay in his palm—cool, dust-coated, streaked with his blood and hers.

His breath caught in his chest.

"Anara…" he whispered. "Tell me this wasn't for nothing."

Silence answered.

Only the low, fading thrum of spacetime settling back into shape, like metal cooling after being bent past breaking.

Rho sank to one knee.

The war had changed shape.

And he wasn't sure if any of them would survive what came next.

Deep beneath where Varos once hung in orbit—under kilometers of fused stone and collapsed tunnels—the pod remained. Untouched. Untouched by heat, gravity, collapse… by anything except the design that had waited for this moment.

Inside, Anara's body floated weightless, hair drifting like smoke in still water. Her eyes were open, fixed on something far beyond the chamber walls.

The glyph pulsed.

Slow

Measured.

Inevitable.

Crystal began to grow along the pod's surface—flowing rather than forming—as if answering ancient instructions only now reactivated. It wrapped the pod in interlocking plates, sealing her into a perfect, unbreakable sarcophagus.

Veins of blue geometry etched themselves across the crystal, glowing like constellations in a forgotten sky.

Then—light.

A projection rose above the tomb.

A shape.

No… a shadow that blocked the stars behind it.

Organic.

Metallic.

Bone-pale.

A Leviathan starship the size of continents.

Older than the war.

Older than the empires that fought it.

Older than the chambers that hid it.

Awakening

Turning.

Listening.

Answering her death.

Something ancient had heard her sacrifice. And it was moving.

It drifted from the dark like a continent of bone, pulling starlight across its hull as if the galaxy itself bent to make room. Ancient plates flexed. Tendrils of cold luminescence rippled down its spine. It had slept through wars, empires, and extinctions. It had forgotten its own name.

But the moment Anara died, it stirred.

It listened.

And it answered.

Slowly—inevitably—it turned its vast, empty gaze toward the system she saved, as if recognizing a summons older than memory.

Something ancient was waking.

And the silence between stars would never be the same.

ABOUT THE AUTHOR

Nicholas Mrvos grew up in Athens, Georgia, and has been a lifelong fan of science fiction, drawn to stories that explore humanity's future, moral complexity, and the cost of progress. He currently lives in the Atlanta area, where he writes speculative fiction that blends hard science, political tension, and character-driven storytelling.

His interests include emerging technologies, philosophy, and the ways innovation reshapes societies—questions that frequently find their way into his work. When not writing, he enjoys reading and traveling.

nicholasmrvos.com

Tiktok: @NicholasMrvosAuthor

Instagram: @NicholasMrvosAuthor

Facebook: @NicholasMrvosAuthor

X: @NicholasMrvos

www.ingramcontent.com/pod-product-compliance
Lightning Source LLC
LaVergne TN
LVHW090558110826
845146LV00001B/183

9798234015570